SAM THOMPSON

WOLFSTONGUE

Illustrated by
ANNA TROMOP

WOLFSTONGUE

First published in 2021 by
Little Island Books
7 Kenilworth Park
Dublin 6w
Ireland

Text © Sam Thompson 2021
Illustrations © Anna Tromop 2021

The author has asserted his moral rights.

A British Library Cataloguing in Publication record for this book is available
from the British Library.

Cover and interior illustrations by Anna Tromop
Cover design and typesetting by Niall McCormack
Proofread by Antoinette Walker
Printed in Turkey by Imago

Print ISBN: 978-1912417759
Ebook (Kindle) ISBN: 978-1912417940
Ebook (other platforms) ISBN: 978-1912417933

Little Island has received funding to support this book from
the Arts Council of Ireland / An Chomhairle Ealaíon

10 9 8 7 6 5 4 3 2 1

For Odhrán

For Sadhbh

For Oisín

You good wolves

Shallow Tunnels

The Gate

Marketplace

Upper Warren

Stone Gardens

GRAND PASSAGE

Middle Burrows

Old Wolf Pens

Lower City Gate

Down Town

Deep Den

Low Plaza

Citadel Gate

Keepers of the Words

City of Earth

Great Hall

CITADEL

The Keep

Deep down and long ago, there are dreams in the clay.

The clay lies deep in the ground. It belongs to a time before living creatures. But the clay dreams of life.

It dreams about running and hunting. It dreams that it will sing, and tell stories, and dance. The clay dreams of shaping itself into creatures that will live and die and dream that once they were clay.

There are dreams in the clay, deep down and long ago.

I

THERE WAS a wolf on the cycle path.

Silas walked along the path every day after school. It ran beside a patch of woodland. It was not the fastest way home, but Silas used it because he liked being by himself, and the cycle path was always empty.

Until today. The wolf stood in the middle of the path, watching him. Its head was as high as his chest. He had never been so close to such a large wild animal.

He did not know what to do. He had seen wolves in a wildlife park once: they had been pale, silent shapes slipping between the trees, too far away to seem dangerous or even quite real. But this wolf was real. He could hear it panting. He could see its wet red tongue and its long white teeth. At the sight, a chill crawled all the way from his shoulders to the base of his spine, and gooseflesh tingled on his arms. His heart beat hard in his chest.

He told himself he ought to back away carefully. He ought to run. *But if I run*, he thought, *the wolf might chase me. Maybe I should flap my arms and shout so that it goes away. Wild animals are usually nervous of people, aren't they?* But the wolf did not look nervous. It looked hungry. Its grey eyes were fixed on Silas, just waiting for him to start running. The narrow path was like a trap, with a brick wall on one side and a wire fence on the other.

He held his breath. He kept very still. And then the wolf took a step forwards.

Silas nearly ran. He nearly cried out in fright and fell over backwards. But he did not do this, not quite, because he had noticed something. The wolf was walking oddly. It was limping, barely touching the ground with one of its front paws. When it was almost within reach, it held up the paw as if it wanted to shake hands.

Silas knelt down beside the wolf. The paw was larger than both his hands together. It had thick grey fur, hard black claws and big rough pads. The smell was strong, but not bad: it was earthy and musky, and it reminded Silas of something. For a moment he could not tell what, but then he knew. The wolf smelled like the scent that rises from dry ground at the end of a hot day when the rain begins to fall.

He moved the pads apart and the wolf growled softly in its throat. Silas let go in a hurry, but the wolf whined and offered him the paw again. Being as slow and gentle as he could, he grasped the paw and tried to see what the matter was. Yes, he thought, something was lodged there. A metallic glint deep between the pads. The wolf gave a snarl as he eased the paw open, but it let him coax the object free. It was an old brass drawing pin, battered and bloody. It must have been digging into the paw at every step.

The wolf circled away and took a few steps along the path, no longer limping.

Then all at once it was alert, lifting its head and swivelling its ears as if it sensed danger. It prowled along the fence until it came to a place where the wire was torn at the bottom, making an entrance into the woodland. The grey eyes locked with Silas's eyes for a moment, and the wolf wriggled through the hole.

The patch of woodland had perhaps twenty trees, with the backs of houses showing through the branches. There was nowhere for a large animal to go. But as Silas watched, the wolf crouched in the undergrowth and disappeared from view.

Silas stood at the fence, wondering if anything else was going to happen. But there was no movement among the trees. It was as if the wolf had never been there. That must be the end, he thought. It had been a brief, strange meeting and now it was time for him to go home.

Then he heard a voice behind him.

'Good afternoon,' it said. 'This *is* a fortunate meeting.'

A fox was sitting on the path: a neat creature with a sharp face and dark red fur. It gazed up at him. Beside it sat a second fox, larger and paler, with green eyes set close together. As Silas watched, more foxes appeared on the path behind the small dark fox and the large pale one. Soon there were twenty foxes sitting and looking at him.

The dark fox spoke.

'My name is Reynard,' he said. 'This is my sister Saffron, and these are our sisters and brothers, and *you* are a very lucky young man. You see, a dangerous animal is on the loose. We're tracking it down, to make sure no one gets hurt.'

The dark fox had large golden eyes. His voice was friendly and calm: the kind of voice you want to trust.

'I have a feeling you've seen the animal we're searching for,' Reynard said. 'And I have an idea you're going to help us.'

Silas did not answer. He was a little surprised that the fox was talking, but not so much as you might think. A talking fox did not seem so strange when it was here in front of him, gazing up with friendly golden eyes. Hearing

4

words come from a fox was really no more strange than hearing them come from a human being.

He wanted to answer but the words would not come. This often happened, especially at school. People spoke to him and waited for a reply, but the words he meant to say got stuck. It had happened today. All through break time Richie Long from his class had followed him around the playground, loudly asking him what his name was. Several other children had joined in too. They knew his name, of course, but they thought it was funny to make him say it. In the end he had tried to tell them to leave him alone, but something in him had seized up, and the words had not come out. Richie Long and the others had laughed and called him the names they always called him: 'Ss-s-s-s-Silas' and 'Silent Silas' and just 'Silence'.

Silence, he thought. He could not deny that the name suited him. He never tried to speak when he could keep quiet instead. And now, in front of Reynard the fox, his words failed again and he said nothing. The pale fox with green eyes snarled and crouched as if she might spring.

'Now, now, Saffron,' Reynard said, 'I'm sure this young man will be only too glad to help us once he understands the situation. You see, young sir, we're searching for a wolf. He doesn't belong here. He's much too big and wild. He's lost, and we only want to help him. So, please: won't you show us where he is?'

Reynard glanced into the woodland, as if he already knew where the wolf had gone. Silas wondered why the foxes were not just pushing under the fence to search among the trees. They seemed to want his help. They wanted to make him part of what they were going to do.

But he did not want to help them find the tired old wolf. He did not understand what was happening between these animals, but he knew that he did not want to see the foxes catch their quarry. He tried not to look at the torn place in the fence. Perhaps he could trick them. He could tell them he had seen a wolf running away towards the other side of town.

He opened his mouth to speak, but it was no good. The words would not come, and all he managed were a few stupid-sounding noises. The pale fox called Saffron showed her teeth. The other foxes looked at one another, as if to say: *What's the matter with this one?* Even Reynard was looking impatient.

'I don't expect you to understand completely,' he said. 'But believe me, if you're wise you will do as I suggest. So now I'm asking one last time. Give me the wolf.'

Silas took a deep breath and tried again to reply: *I don't know where he is, and I wouldn't tell you if I did.* That was what he wanted to say. But no words came. A couple of the foxes giggled.

Reynard twitched his tail.

'This child is of no use to us,' he said.

He lifted his nose, and all the foxes got up.

'Not yet, anyway,' Reynard added, as his followers vanished along the cycle path.

The last fox to leave was the one called Saffron. Before she went, she walked over to Silas, like a pet coming to sniff at his knee. He looked down to see what she wanted.

The next thing Silas knew was pain: sickening, searing, frightening pain. It began in his left ankle and burst through his entire body. The fox had bitten him. He was too astonished to react. The thin blades of her teeth were still buried deep in the sinew above his heel. As she bit down, the fox lashed her head from side to side. She kept her eyes on his face as if she wanted to know how much it hurt.

'Saffron!' said Reynard. He was standing some way along the path. 'Come along.'

The pale fox rolled her eyes and let go. She followed Reynard, licking her jaws.

Silas was alone. Crying and shaking with the pain, he sank to the ground, grasping his ankle. His hands were covered in blood.

2

SILAS TOOK off his shoe and gently peeled away the blood-soaked sock from his wounded ankle. The pain was quite different from a scrape or a cut: it throbbed up his leg as if some burning substance had been poured into his veins. This pain was telling him that real damage had been done, that something was wrong deep inside and would not easily be put right. Forcing himself to look, he saw the blood welling from a ragged tear in his flesh. His foot and ankle were turning an ugly purplish black and already beginning to swell, the skin stretching smooth like the surface of a balloon.

Silas gritted his teeth and tried to wrap his handkerchief around his ankle. It did little to stop the blood and it hurt more than he could bear. He tried to stand up, but the pain made him sob and he slid back to the ground.

Something moved in the undergrowth. He saw a grey muzzle. Slowly, the wolf came out: a hungry, bony shadow, making no noise as it passed among the trees. Silas gripped the fence and hauled himself upright. The wolf pushed under the wire, padded towards him and sniffed at his ankle.

Then the wolf spoke.

'This is a bad bite,' he said. 'Can you walk?'

Silas stared at the wolf, bewildered. He was really scared, now, that the blood would not stop flowing: the handkerchief was already dark red and sopping wet.

'If you can't walk, you can ride,' said the wolf. 'It's not far, but we must hurry. The foxes will come back.'

Silas tried to speak, and the tears stung his eyes as, again, he failed. The wolf watched. Silas dug his nails into his palms and at last forced the words out, one by one.

'You ... talk?'

The wolf growled and turned his head away. Silas did not understand why, but he felt that he had said something wrong or that he had been rude by mistake. He felt sure the wolf was going to walk off down the path and disappear for good.

But the wolf did not leave. He paused, his head hanging low, and at last he spoke again.

'My name is Isengrim,' he said.

'Silas,' said Silas. The word came a little more easily this time.

Isengrim crouched, pressing his belly to the ground.

'Very well, Silas,' he said. 'Can you hold tight?'

A few moments later Silas was digging his fingers into Isengrim's fur as the wolf loped along the path. The weight of a boy on his back did not seem to slow him down, and soon they were moving faster than Silas could run. Concrete, fence and hedge streamed past, then garden walls and the backs of allotments. Silas clung on.

Ahead lay the end of the cycle path, where he would usually pass through a row of bollards on his way home. But now they did not reach the bollards, because Isengrim dived sideways, without slowing down, as if he meant to slam into the brick wall that ran beside them.

Silas flinched, expecting an impact, but none came. When he opened his eyes they were plunging along a passage with walls of mossy brick. He had never noticed the turning before.

Dead leaves kicked up around them, and several times the wolf leaped over big dry branches blocking the way. The walls drew closer together and the moss thickened so that no more brick could be seen. Isengrim did not slow down. Silas tried not to cry out at the jolting pain in his ankle.

Then, all of a sudden, they were out of the passage and into somewhere else.

They were surrounded by trees. But not scrawny trees like those beside the cycle path. Everywhere, thick, twisted, mossy trunks reached up and tangled their arms into a canopy. Fallen branches hung in nets of creepers. The ground was a mass of roots. Leaves dripped. Silas looked back over his shoulder, trying to see how they had left the city behind, but all he could see was green twilight, great ferns and trunks flashing past. It was like racing through a maze of tunnels in some underground place.

Isengrim slowed to a trot. The ordinary atmosphere of the city – its stale and reheated air, its low grumble of traffic, its thin cloudy light – had been whisked away like a dust sheet. Silas's senses were vibrating with the discovery that light, sound and smell could all merge together in one great glow. All around him the scent that breathed from the trees curled like mist, softening the sunlight and scattering it among the branches. Swaying shadows and leaves made droplets of brightness and an endless whispering that wove with the warbling of birds to a vast hush, a sound bigger and deeper than silence. The smell of the air, so fresh and fine, was like a promise that something was about to happen; and that something was everything. Silas felt he could breathe it in for ever.

The trees grew thinner. The wolf came to a halt, and they looked out over the land. In front of them a rocky slope dropped down to a band of loose stones. Beyond that the woods began again. The landscape spread below was one enormous forest, reaching to the horizon. The green beneath them was broken only by a spur of rock here and a glimmer of water there.

All Silas could think was that they had come into another world.

Isengrim sniffed the air.

'There's only one world,' he said.

The wolf sped up again, running along the ridge, an inch from the drop, sure-footed. Silas, confused, dug his fingers deeper in the hot fur. He must have spoken aloud without realising it, he thought.

'This is the Forest,' Isengrim said as he ran. 'Your species lives here too. You just don't notice, most of the time.'

Then he leaped over the edge. A line of boulders lay in a broken diagonal down the scarp. Silas would not have been able to get down such a steep and jagged slope by himself, but Isengrim jumped easily from rock to rock.

A little way into the woodland at the bottom, they came to a place where a huge old tree had fallen long ago. The trunk lay along the forest floor and the root ball hung, exposed, above the socket from which it had been torn.

'This is my home,' said the wolf.

They pushed through hanging ivy, into the hollow under the roots.

'And here is my family.'

Another wolf stood waiting for them in the hollow. This one was a little smaller than Isengrim: her limbs lighter, the features of her face finer, her ears and muzzle tipped with a paler grey. Silas slid from Isengrim's back and collapsed. The wolves circled, pushing their noses into the fur at one another's throats. They rubbed their faces together.

When they had finished their greetings, the other wolf looked at Silas. Her eyes were grey and clear as ice.

'He's fox-bitten,' said Isengrim.

The other wolf disappeared into the darkness under the tree roots. The hole went deep, Silas saw. It had been dug out to make a den. He tried to make himself more comfortable on the ground, but the pain was even worse now. His foot was a swollen lump, a great weight of agony dangling from his leg, and he dared not look at it. The burning numbness seemed to be spreading, forcing its threads up through his body all the way to his chest and throat.

The other wolf came back, holding something in her mouth. It was part of a large fish, perhaps a salmon. She laid it in front of Isengrim, who growled.

'I'm fine,' he said. 'See to the child.'

But the wolf's voice was faint, and Silas saw he was exhausted. He looked even more worn out than when they had met on the path. Without another word Isengrim lay down and began to gnaw at the dark, shrivelled meat of the fish.

The other wolf disappeared into the darkness again and returned carrying something else in her jaws. She dropped it at Silas's feet. It was a lump of clay.

'My name is Hersent,' she said. 'Now show me that bite.'

The clay was blue-black. Tiny bright specks twinkled in it, like stars in a handful of night sky. Hersent began to work the lump in her mouth, softening it.

Silas was growing light-headed. He felt himself dissolving into a jumble of sickness and confusion as the wolf peeled away his bloody handkerchief and pressed the clay to the place where the fox had bitten him. Hersent licked and smoothed the clay, and a wonderful coolness began to soak through his ankle.

'Rest a while,' she said.

Silas closed his eyes.

He did not know how much time passed as he lay under the roof of roots, half drowsing and half hearing as Isengrim told Hersent the story of what had happened to him. How the foxes had surprised the wolf while he was out searching for food, and how he had fled for three days and nights without rest, unable to shake them off, until a sharp thing got stuck in his paw and he found that he could not run any longer. How he had been close to surrender when he was saved by the human child.

The wolves went on talking for a long time. Isengrim's voice was low and serious, and he sounded as if it hurt him to be talking at all. Hersent spoke more than he did, and faster: she sounded angry. But what the wolves said, Silas did not know, because he was growing ever drowsier. And soon he slept.

He dreamed.

In the dream he was not himself. He was not a living creature. He was blue-black clay that lay buried deep down in the ground. The dream was happening a long time ago, he felt: so long ago that there were no living creatures yet in the world. There was only the clay deep in the ground, waiting for life, dreaming that some day it would shape itself into creatures that would run on the earth. He was the clay, and the dream ran through him, and sometimes the dream was shaped like a boy, and sometimes it was shaped like a wolf.

———•=•———

When he woke the sky was dark and Isengrim was standing over him. The clay on his ankle had dried and crumbled. He brushed away the dust to find his skin was whole again. It was marked with pale scars but it did not hurt.

'I'll lead you back,' Isengrim said.

Hersent was lying on her side in the shelter of the roots.

'Keep away from foxes,' she said. 'That was the last of our clay.'

Silas nodded. He would have liked to thank the wolves for helping him, but he knew he would not be able to get the words out. He only stood at the mouth of the den and waved a clumsy farewell. Then he paused, noticing something. Hersent's middle was swollen beneath the fur. He remembered what Isengrim had said about a family.

As if she guessed what he was thinking, Hersent gave a friendly growl.

'They're due any day now,' she said.

Isengrim padded back to his mate and nuzzled her belly.

'Hersent and I are the last wolves left in the Forest,' he said. 'But soon there will be more of us.'

3

THE NEXT morning, Silas kept thinking of the wolves.

After leaving the den, he had followed Isengrim through the woodland, tripping on roots and ducking under branches. He had felt as though he were walking on the bed of an ocean whose depths were the whispering fathoms of the forest canopy, reaching far above, raining their gentle scent and filling with green shadows at the end of the day. One moment the twilight Forest had seemed endless around him, but the next they had pushed through a clump of bushes and were standing on a quiet street, ten minutes' walk from Silas's house. Isengrim had left him there, vanishing silently into the shadow of a hedge.

Now it was hard to feel sure those things had happened. That he had been bitten by a fox and healed by a wolf, or that he had found a vast forest hidden around the corners of the places he knew. As he walked to school the streets were no different from usual. At the school gate, a large raven was watching him from a fence post, but then a tabby cat leaped onto the fence and the bird flapped away in alarm. Nothing seemed out of the ordinary.

At break time he sat on a bench at the edge of the playground, away from the shouts and shrieks, and put a hand down his sock to feel the dents where the bite had healed. There was a lot to think about. His head was full of dripping leaves and deep glades and distant mountains. He could feel the wolves moving silently through that landscape. Isengrim had explained that the Forest was everywhere, and that you could find ways into it anywhere you chose to look for them. Silas wondered if he could get there again.

A hand waved in front of his face.

'Hello? Anyone at home?'

Voices laughed.

Silas looked up, confused. His thoughts were still with the wolves in the Forest.

'Hey, Silence,' someone said, 'why are you sitting by yourself?'

Richie Long was a large boy with orange hair and a wide fleshy mouth. He was the same age as Silas, but with his thick neck and brawny arms he looked older. He was always ready to barge his weight into Silas, to knock him down or flatten him against a wall, and he never came by himself. Today, three of his sidekicks were standing a little way off, smirking and waiting to join in. For no obvious reason, one of the boys gave another one a shove and got punched in return.

Richie Long leaned over Silas.

'Why aren't you talking to anyone?'

Silas didn't answer. He wanted to explain that he was happy sitting here by himself, but the words were too hard to find.

'What's that?' said Richie Long, cupping a hand to his ear. 'I didn't quite catch that.'

The three boys were beginning to snigger. Richie Long's mouth stretched into a grin. Silas looked away. He noticed that the tabby cat was on the wall, watching. One of its ears was damaged.

'I think he's trying to tell us something,' said Richie Long. 'Go on, Silence, you can do it.'

The boys were crowding Silas. He looked down at his shoes.

'I mean, what is wrong with you?' Richie Long said. 'How can you actually be this stupid?'

He sounded angry, but his grin was still widening. Silas tried once more to find what he had to say, to force the words out. But nothing came.

'Let's try something easy,' said Richie Long. He breathed cheesy fumes in Silas's face, and spoke very loudly and slowly.

'WHAT ... IS ... YOUR ... NAME?'

Silas shrank down on the bench, cringing away from the great laughing mouth, knowing what a loser he must look. Then he pushed himself off the seat and past the boys. As he went, one of them shoved him hard in the shoulder so that he staggered and almost fell. The voices cheered and called after him as he walked away.

He did not care where he was going. Aloneness closed around him, cool and soothing, as he followed a track that ran behind the main school building and past a cupboard where the sports equipment was kept. Soon the playground voices were far away. They were much less real than the flowing of the trees in the wind and the rustlings in the bushes.

Those boys made fun of him every break and he did not know what to do about it. He knew you were meant to tell a grown-up if you were having trouble like this, but it was impossible. If he spoke to a teacher, his words would stumble and stick until he gave up. And telling his parents would be even worse. He could picture their looks of disappointment as he tried to make them understand. They thought he was just a bit shy and slow, and that was bad enough. He could not bear to think how hurt they would be if they discovered that he could not even speak when he was away from them. He knew by now that the best thing he could do, at home and at school, was to open his mouth as little as possible, draw no attention to himself and hope no-one noticed that he was hiding away.

He did not know whether he was allowed down here. The track ended at a large shed with cobwebbed windows. The padlock hung open. He slipped inside.

As his eyes got used to the dimness, he made out paint cans on shelves, piled sacks, garden tools, a lawnmower. He smelled creosote, grass cuttings and petrol. He knew he must not stay long. They would say he had run away and hidden. But he was not ready to go back yet. He stood in the cool, smelly space and took ten deep breaths, in and out.

When he stepped outside again, foxes were everywhere. The empty track had come alive with small sharp teeth and bristling backs in every shade of orange and brown. They swarmed from the hedges and the bushes. They snapped at him and drove him back into the shed.

The door banged shut. Reflecting eyes were all around him.

'Please, don't leave yet,' said Reynard the fox. 'We have so much to talk about.'

Several of the foxes were dragging an old classroom chair into the middle of the room.

'Have a seat,' said Reynard. 'Please.'

Silas sat down in the cracked plastic seat. Strong jaws seized his hands and skilful jaws looped lengths of gardening wire around them, so that, before he knew it, his wrists were tied to the metal frame.

'We've been watching you today, Silas.'

Reynard's voice was soft and friendly.

'We've been waiting to have a conversation,' he said. 'Yesterday you weren't helpful. But today I think you will be. I think you know where the wolves are hiding.'

One of the foxes jumped up to his lap. With a sick lurch of his stomach, he recognised the fox who had bitten him in the ankle. There was a gleam of anticipation in her green eyes.

'Of course,' said Reynard, 'I may be wrong. You may know nothing. That is possible. But, regrettably, we have no time to waste on the question. So what's going to happen is this. My sister Saffron, here, is going to eat her dinner.'

Saffron licked her chops. Her breath streamed hot in Silas's face, stinking of spoiled meat. He wanted to draw back, but he could not, because the needle-sharp teeth of the fox were gripping the flesh of his cheek. It was only a pinch, not yet enough to draw blood.

'Saffron has an excellent appetite, I can assure you,' Reynard said. 'And she will keep on eating until you give us the wolves.'

The green eye was staring directly into his eye, bright with wicked delight.

'Anything you'd like to tell us?' Reynard asked. 'No? Very well, then.'

Saffron's teeth pricked his skin – but then the door crashed open, and a big dark shape showed against the daylight.

It was Isengrim.

Scared though he was of the foxes, Silas felt a thrill of deeper, more instinctive terror at the enormous animal that crouched in the doorway with his teeth bared and a growl rolling in his throat. The foxes scattered to the far corners of the shed. Even Saffron darted behind a pile of buckets. Only Reynard did not move. He sat and waited as Isengrim padded towards him.

When they were nose to nose, the wolf looming over the fox, Isengrim's growl became a saw-toothed snarl. Silas could not understand why Reynard did not run for his life.

But then the fox spoke.

'Naughty wolf,' he said.

The snarl faltered, and Isengrim's ear twitched.

'Bad, stupid wolf,' Reynard said. 'When will you learn?'

He tutted.

'I have tracked down this slow-witted human child to find out where you're hiding. And what do you do? You turn up and save me the trouble. I'd have expected more sense, even from you.'

Isengrim flicked his ears as if a fly were bothering him.

'And while you're here, who's taking care of the good lady Hersent?' Reynard said. 'I'm shocked at you, leaving her alone in her delicate condition. Oh, yes. I'm well aware of her condition.'

Isengrim's snarl died away.

'Poor old Isengrim,' Reynard said. 'You don't know what you're doing.'

Isengrim seemed to be getting smaller as Reynard spoke. His shoulders and tail sagged. Silas was not sure what was happening, but it was clear that the fox was exerting some influence over the wolf. With every word, Reynard sounded more commanding. Silas longed to interrupt, to tell Isengrim not to listen, but his throat seemed to have closed entirely. He could not make a sound.

'Once you were a big, strong beast,' Reynard said. 'But now you're tired, worn out and weak. You're no use to anyone.'

Isengrim drew back the corners of his mouth in a kind of unhappy grin. If only he could say something now, Silas knew, he could stop this. He strained until the wires cut his wrists, trying to get the words out by sheer desperation, but all he produced was a faint, foolish choking sound.

'Ah well,' said Reynard. 'It's worked out for the best.'

The other foxes had their courage back by now and were edging towards Isengrim. They seemed to have forgotten about Silas.

'You're back with your masters,' Reynard was saying, 'and that's all that need concern you. So be a good old wolf and lie down.'

Isengrim did as he was told, settling his head between his front legs. Seeing this, Saffron darted close and swatted him in the nose with her paw.

'Good,' said Reynard. 'This old wolf obeys his masters as is right and proper. Soon we'll bring in the other runaway too.'

The wolf closed his eyes wearily.

But then he opened them again at the sound of a voice that had not yet spoken.

'Isengrim!' it called.

It took Silas a long moment to understand that the voice was his own. He had said the wolf's name so loudly and clearly that his whole chest was still tingling. His throat felt open, unlocked. Astonished, he carried on.

'Why ... why are you letting him speak to you like that?'

The wolf blinked dully at Silas.

'The things he's saying aren't true,' Silas said. 'You aren't ... bad or stupid or weak.'

Isengrim's ears lifted.

'I mean – you came here to help me, didn't you? That wasn't stupid. That was brave and kind.'

Isengrim raised his head from the floor. The foxes drew back, uneasy.

'And you're not weak, either,' said Silas. 'You're strong. When I couldn't walk, you put me on your back and ran for miles. And when I was hurt, you helped me. So, saying you're no use to anyone is a lie!'

Isengrim got to his feet, and he was no longer cringing.

His mane bristled.

'And – and I don't see why these foxes should tell you what to do,' said Silas.

He was not quite sure what he wanted to say, but he kept going anyway, afraid that if he slowed down or thought about it, the power of speech might desert him as suddenly as it had come.

'I think they're just being mean,' he said. 'And I don't think you should let them.'

He knew he would not be able to carry on much longer. Any moment now he would hesitate or trip over a word, and then he would go back to being as tongue-tied as ever. He took a deep breath, determined to get at least a few more words out, hoping they would be enough.

'Isengrim,' he said, 'don't let them tell you what to do.'

Silas felt a vibration: a sound so low that it was almost beneath hearing, seeming to rise up from the concrete floor through the soles of his feet to judder his bones. It was the snarl gathering again, deep in Isengrim's throat. The sound rose until the paint cans rattled on the shelves and the tools swayed on their hooks. Isengrim advanced on Reynard. The wolf, a great dark bulk of strength and rage, his muzzle a mask of teeth, bore down on the small, graceful figure of the fox.

The other foxes had slipped away, but Reynard still sat there, gazing calmly at a set of jaws that could take off his head with one snap. Silas was suddenly afraid of what the wolf might do next. Above all, he did not want to see anyone get hurt: he did not think he could cope with any more blood and pain.

'Isengrim?' he said.

The wolf's eyes flickered to Silas. It was only an instant of distraction, but that was long enough for Reynard to dodge past and vanish.

Wolf and boy looked at the doorway where the fox had escaped, and Isengrim roared in fury. He swung his huge head around, fangs bared. Silas was aware, too late, that he was the only creature left here at the mercy of an enraged predator. Terror ran through him, pure and cold. But then the snarl died and the lips closed over the teeth. The animal, which briefly had been nothing but a murderous beast, was Isengrim again.

The wolf came to the boy and bit through the wire that bound him.

THE RAVEN was perched in a tree beside the shed, watching with a beady black eye. Isengrim lifted his nose towards the bird in a gesture of greeting.

'*Kraa*,' she said. 'A friend of the wolves is a friend of mine.'

'Oh, they're gone, are they?' said another voice.

The tabby cat with the ragged ear was sitting on the roof of the shed. His face was a smile behind his whiskers.

'Good,' he said. 'They get on my nerves.'

The raven's name was Corax, and the cat was called Tybalt. Silas gathered that both of them had helped to save him from the foxes.

'Saw them trap you, human child,' Corax said. 'Flew fast. Found the grey wolf.'

'It was well done,' Isengrim said.

'Raven always knows where to find a wolf,' Corax said. 'Fox almost caught me, but the cat clawed it and I got away.'

'Let's not make a big thing of it, birdy,' Tybalt said. 'Those foxes were going to eat you, is all, and I won't have that. I'm going to eat you myself one of these days.'

'Oh, you're always joking,' Corax said. 'Eat me. As if!'

The cat narrowed his eyes at the raven.

'Come to think of it ...'

Without further warning, he bunched his body and leaped, landing on the branch where Corax had been sitting a moment before. But now she was flapping into the air. She cawed a farewell that sounded like laughter – *kraa kraa* – as she spiralled upwards and away.

'Oh well,' Tybalt said. 'Catch you next time, then.'

He yawned, stretched and shivered.

'This has been fine,' he said, 'but I have a number of more exciting places to be.'

The cat strolled along the branch and jumped out of sight.

'So they don't like the foxes either,' Silas said.

'The foxes have made many enemies,' Isengrim said. 'And now you are their enemy too. We have to leave.'

'Leave?' said Silas. He could no longer hear the distant voices in the playground. Break time must have finished. He should be back in the classroom.

'I'll explain as we travel,' said Isengrim.

Silas could not understand how they got into the Forest. Isengrim did no more than lead him down the side of the shed, under a low branch, and all at once they were in ancient woodland. Behind lay the rear of the building and the path to the playground. In front, an endlessness of trees where the air opened and the earth breathed. Mossy trunks, trickling of water and stirrings of birds.

'How did we get here?' he said. 'I still can't work it out.'

But Isengrim was already leading into the woods. Silas followed through the mesh of branches, roots and ferns.

As they went, Isengrim told him the story of the wolves and the foxes.

Once, Isengrim explained, there had been many wolves. They had lived in packs, travelling and hunting together in every part of the Forest. No-one knew how many wolves there were, because numbers meant nothing to the wolves in those days. And no one knew how long those days lasted, because the wolves did not keep track of time. The wolves of the Forest travelled and hunted together, and that was all.

But one day the foxes came. The foxes were smaller than the wolves and less fierce. They should have been frightened and stayed away. But instead they did something that was new to the wolves. They spoke.

Reynard the fox came to one of the wolves and he said: *Your name shall be Isengrim.*

'He gave me my name,' Isengrim told Silas. 'Before that, I could have ignored him. Or I could have ended him with one blow of my paw. But after he gave me a name, I had to listen.'

So the foxes gave names to the wolves, and taught them how to speak. Words were a gift, the foxes said. Before they had words, the wolves had been wild animals, but now they were more than that.

And Isengrim felt this was true. He looked at the trees of the Forest and said to himself: *Those are the trees.* He looked at rock and river and sky, and said these names too. For the first time, he looked at the other wolves of his pack and knew who they were. There was Snow, named for his white fur; Skip, who loved to jump and play; Pilgrim, so called because she had journeyed further through the Forest than any other wolf.

Isengrim looked at his mate, and said, *Hersent*, and she looked at him and said, *Isengrim*, and they knew one another in a way they had not known before. He felt that the foxes had given a wonderful gift to the wolves.

Isengrim looked at Reynard and said to himself: *This is my friend.*

But something was wrong for the wolves. There had always been hardship: winters were cold, bellies went empty, and often enough wolves would die of injury or sickness. But it seemed to Isengrim that he had never really felt these hardships before the foxes came. Now the cold and hunger hurt his body in a way they had not done before, and the loss of those wolves that died hurt him inside in a way he could not understand.

What was happening to Isengrim happened to the other wolves as well. Until the foxes taught them the words for sadness and fear, they had not known what it was to be sad and afraid. But now they knew, and because of this they began to lose their strength. They were filled with doubt. Fewer wolf pups were born, and those that did come were sickly and small. Wolves grew old and ill and died before their time.

Soon the wolves went to the foxes.

'Please help us,' they said. 'You gave us words, but now we are sad and afraid and we don't know why. Please tell us what we should do.'

Reynard was there, leading the foxes.

'Very well,' he said. 'You need not worry any longer. We will tell you what to do.'

And after that, everything changed for the wolves.

What Reynard told them was that the foxes were building a city. Like any foxes' dwelling, it was a burrow under the ground, but this was to be a burrow on a grand scale. It would reach for miles beneath the forest floor, and it would not be a place of earth, roots, tunnels and holes. It would be a true city, built of brick and iron and glass. It would be like no place ever seen in the Forest.

To build such a place would need hard labour, and this the wolves would supply. It was a small price for what the foxes offered in return. They would give the wolves food and shelter, so that they would never again have to range through the Forest, cold and hungry, on the hunt. Best of all, they would tell the wolves what to do, so they would never have to decide for themselves.

So Isengrim and Hersent and the other wolves built the foxes' city. They spent their days digging in darkness or hauling loads of earth up to the surface. Foxes barked instructions and nipped them when they were too slow. Other animals worked for the foxes too: the mule named

Baldwin, who dragged cartfuls of timber and stone from far parts of the Forest, and the old bear, Bruno, who could lift rocks too heavy for any other beast. At the end of each day the wolves would lie exhausted in their pens and eat the slops and bones the foxes gave them.

Isengrim did not know how much time passed in this way. He was too tired to tell.

Once, during those days, a wolf ran away. It was Snow, the wolf named for his white fur. He had not given any clue that he was planning an attempt, but one day he escaped into the Forest. He was gone for two days and nights, and a quiet excitement began to stir among the wolves. Isengrim felt that he was waking up from a long sleep. Then, on the third day, the foxes brought Snow back with dark stains on his whiteness. He was dead. They hung his body up in the Marketplace, where all the animals of the city passed, and left it there until it was nothing but bones.

At last the foxes declared their city finished. Its name, they said, was the Earth. As they had promised, it was magnificent. The tunnels were paved with stone and walled with brick. The light of oil lamps spilled along spacious underground streets and glimmered in the windows of the fine houses where the foxes would live from now on. There were galleries and halls, markets and courts, shops and gardens, and at the heart of the city lay a buried palace.

The wolves had worked hard to build the city and many had died of the strain. Surely, Isengrim thought, now that the city was built the few wolves that were left would be allowed to rest. But it was not so. In the finished city there was as much work for the wolves as ever. The foxes kept thinking of improvements – a wider avenue here, a new underground mansion there – and this meant that Isengrim must carry on hauling cart-loads of earth, day after day. While he did this, Hersent walked in one of the treadmills that the foxes had invented to draw up water from deep underground.

So the wolves worked for the foxes, and as they worked, they died. They died because their work was too hard, and their food was too poor, and because they could think of no reason not to.

Until only two wolves were left. On the night that Isengrim and Hersent realised they were the only ones, they made up their minds. They began to make plans and watch for chances. Whenever they could, they eavesdropped on the talk of their masters, until they knew which routes through the city were left unguarded, and when. They gathered their courage in secret and built up their strength.

Then, one night, they broke the lock of their pen. They crept through low, twisting tunnels until they came to the Grand Passage, the broad thoroughfare that curled all the way from the bottom of the foxes' city to the top. The wolves had dug it themselves, and they knew that it was the fastest way out of the city. They also knew that the foxes would never expect them to set foot there. They stole through the shadows.

When they reached the surface, they saw something they had not seen for longer than they could remember. It rode unveiled in the cornerless sky. It silvered clouds and branches. It was the moon.

———◆———

'And since then,' Isengrim said, 'we run and hide.'

They had been pushing through the woodland, and now they came to a place Silas knew. A giant tree lay fallen. Isengrim trotted to the torn-up roots. At the entrance to the den he paused.

'It was an unlucky day for you when you met me, and came to the attention of the foxes,' he said. 'Foxes do not forget those who have crossed them. They won't leave you alone now, and so our lots are joined together. You need our help and we need yours.'

Inside the den, Hersent lifted her head and gave a friendly whine. She did not get up. As his eyes got used to the gloom, Silas saw the reason. Three tiny wolf pups, each small enough to lie on the palm of a hand, lay nuzzled into their mother's belly.

'We need your help now, most of all,' said Isengrim.

5

'ONCE, WHEN the Forest was young,' said Hersent, 'there was a wolf.'

Rain was pattering on the leaves outside. Silas sat cross-legged under the roof of knotted roots, breathing in the warm stink of the den, watching the pups. They were three small handfuls of fluff, less than a day old. Isengrim lay beside Hersent and licked them as they snuffled for their milk. Outside it was cold and wet, but in here it was dry and Hersent was telling a story.

'One day,' she said, 'the wolf got caught in a snare. Try as he might he could not free himself. Not far away, a human child was passing through the woods, and she heard the wolf's distress. She followed the noise and saw that the wolf was trapped. She crept close and undid the snare, and the wolf ran away.'

'But in helping the wolf the human child had strayed from her path. She wandered further from home, growing cold and hungry and ever more lost. Eventually the child lay down in despair.

'It was not long before the wolf crossed the path the child had taken, and he caught the scent of her lostness. Soon he found her where she was lying. He took her on his back and carried her to a place where water ran and blackberries grew, and she ate and drank.

'After that, the wolf's strong back carried the child when her feet grew tired, and his sharp teeth hunted for them both. The child watched for the signs that human hunters make to mark their traps, so the wolf would never be caught by them again.

'And so,' murmured Hersent, 'the wolf and the child travelled far through the Forest together, and they became true companions.'

She licked her pups.

'They're asleep,' Isengrim said.

Silas leaned closer.

'What are they? I mean, boys or girls?'

'Three females,' Hersent said. 'Touch them if you like.'

He stroked the tiny animals, wondering why it was so easy to speak when he was here in the wolves' den. In the warm darkness and the earthy reek, his words were coming more freely than they ever had before. Isengrim had explained that in here they were as safe from the foxes as they could be anywhere, because foxes never came into another creature's home unless they were invited.

Outside the rain was steady. The afternoon had grown dim. Silas could barely make out the shapes of the wolves, but he felt the sleepy heat that came from their bodies.

'What are they called?' he said.

Hersent growled.

'They have no names,' Isengrim said. 'Nor will they.'

'We have names because the foxes gave them to us,' said Hersent. 'But wolves ought not to have names, and these three will live nameless.'

One of the pups lifted her head and yawned. Her eyes were sealed shut.

Then a shock went through both wolves and in a single movement they were on their feet, crouched and alert. At first Silas could not tell why, but then he heard it, behind the hiss and clatter of the rain. Voices were calling.

'*Iiiiisengrim ...*'

'*Herrrrsent ...*'

'Where are you, old fellow?'

'Come out, dear lady!'

'We've come to pay our respects.'

'We have gifts for the babies.'

'We're here for the christening.'

'Aren't you going to invite us in?'

'No need to be shy.'

'We know you're there!'

Isengrim snarled.

'I was sure we weren't followed,' he said. 'I'm an old fool.'

'No time for that,' Hersent said. 'What now?'

The wolves were keeping very still.

'They won't come in,' Isengrim said. 'But they're too clever. Sooner or later they'll trick us into coming out. And if they can't do that, they'll wait for us to starve.'

'Then we leave,' Hersent said.

Isengrim was at the mouth of the den, where rain splattered.

'They're close,' he said.

'Quickly, then.'

Hersent nosed at the pups and said: 'Silas. Your coat.'

Silas took off his jacket. Following Hersent's instructions, he spread it on the ground and filled it with the dried leaves and moss that carpeted the den. She lifted the pups into the middle of this nest, then gathered the corners of the jacket in her jaws, making a bundle with her pups held inside.

She carried the bundled pups into the rear of the den and vanished. Silas could not see where she had gone.

'You next,' said Isengrim.

Silas ducked under a root and found himself wriggling

upwards into a space that was dark, cold and tight. Damp wood pressed on him. The rain battered all around. Ahead, he could make out movement in the darkness as Hersent crawled along what seemed to be a tunnel.

The big fallen tree was hollow. They were inside the trunk.

Silas squirmed forwards on his stomach, but the space narrowed until he was wedged tight. He wriggled and strained but got nowhere. His heart beat hard against the wood.

'Be calm,' said Isengrim, somewhere behind him. 'If we can pass, so can you.'

And it was true that the wolves seemed to have no trouble fitting through. Hersent's claws were scrabbling on the wood, somewhere ahead. Silas shut his eyes, breathed out, found a toe-hold and twisted forwards. Just then a smudge of light appeared in the darkness, and he saw the tip of Hersent's tail disappearing down through a knothole.

He followed – and landed face down in mud. Rainfall roared in the leaves. His eyes and mouth were full of water. He spat, coughed and struggled to his knees, his clothes soaked, as Isengrim dropped down beside him. They were among the branches of the fallen tree.

Hersent set off into the woods, carrying the bundled jacket in her jaws.

'Oh *woo*-holves!' The voice was almost lost in the rain.

But the next one sounded closer: 'Where *aaare* you?'

They ran. Branches whipped Silas's face and brambles dragged at his legs. He ran with his head down, with no idea of where he was going, trying to keep up with the loping grey shapes. The ground began to slope downwards, first gently and then more steeply, until Silas was half running and half falling, his shoes slithering down channels of mud, unable to stop. A thorned branch took his legs out from under him so that he slid twenty feet on his side and came to rest sitting waist-deep in a stream.

Cold bit his flesh so hard that he could not breathe. The stream flowed fast around him, brown with the silt the rain had stirred. His lungs were raw, and he had bitten his tongue. Isengrim stood at the top of the far bank. Gasping, Silas splashed to his feet and clawed his way up through the mud and brambles and blinding rain.

A short time later Silas and the wolves huddled in the shelter of a rock. It was a lump of stone sticking up from the forest floor, almost buried in ivy but offering enough of an overhang to keep the rain off. Silas's teeth knocked together. His jeans and sweater were now a single suit of muck, clinging to his body. The wolves were not nearly so bedraggled: their coats were made of two different sorts of fur, Silas noticed, and while the long, coarse hairs now glistened with wetness, the short, dense fur underneath was dry.

Hersent laid her bundle down and teased it open. The three tiny creatures stirred comfortably. One of them lifted her nose towards her mother.

'We can rest here a few minutes,' Isengrim said. 'No longer.'

Silas shivered, sniffed and tried to rub some of the water out of his hair. His hip-bone ached where he had fallen. His jeans stuck to his legs, clammy and stiff. All at once he was homesick: a longing so intense that it shocked him like the freezing stream. Where was he? How had he ended up here? He wondered how long it had been since he followed the wolf into the trees. Maybe school was over and it was evening already. Maybe his parents and his sister were already home: Mum and Dad standing in the kitchen talking about the news or whose turn it was to make the dinner, Allie busy on her phone. Soon someone would go to the foot of the stairs, call his name and begin to wonder why he was not coming down.

He did not belong in this Forest of foxes and wolves. He was a human being, made for hot showers, electric light and central heating. He needed to be with his family in his own warm, dry house.

'Home,' he said, stumbling over the word. 'I have to go.'

He glanced around the bleak shelter, at the dripping ivy, the sheet of rain to one side of him and the lichen-streaked stone on the other. There was no comfort here, no escape from the cold and the wet.

Then he gave a start, because a face was looking back at him. It was a flat, round face, a person's face, and for a weird moment he thought it was alive and grinning at him. But it was only a decoration carved into the stone. The face was surrounded by carved leaves which sprouted from its cheeks, chin and eyebrows, as if the person were half human and half tree. The carving was pitted and worn, but there was mischief in the stone features. Silas looked again at the shelter. It was not a single rock, after all. He saw flat surfaces where stones had been cut, and straight lines where they had been joined.

They were sheltering in the ruins of something that had been built, long ago, by people.

'Speaking of home, I need to ask you something,' Isengrim said.

He paused and growled softly. If Silas had not known better he would have thought the great grey wolf was embarrassed.

'Do you, by any chance,' Isengrim said, 'have a spare room?'

6

SILAS DID not tell anyone about the wolves in his attic.

They had made their den beside an old wardrobe, hidden behind some broken furniture and mouldy cardboard boxes. Whenever Silas could slip away without his parents or sister noticing, he stole up to the attic to visit. It was like having a secret treasure. The pups were still helpless bundles of warm fur, huddled into their mother, but each time he saw them they were bigger.

'Look,' Hersent whispered one day.

Silas leaned into the gap beside the wardrobe. Three pairs of eyes gazed up, pale blue and brand new.

'They opened this morning,' Hersent said.

As Silas stroked the pups, Isengrim appeared through the hatch that led to the space under the roof slates. This was the wolves' way in and out of the attic: the low, long roof space ran along the whole row of houses, making a tunnel through which a wolf could crawl without anyone noticing. From the end of the row, Silas guessed, they must have some hidden way to get outside and into the Forest.

Snowflakes hung in Isengrim's fur. He padded to Hersent, opened his mouth as if he were being sick and brought up a mound of dark red stuff. It dropped on the floorboards, and she gobbled it up. The pups were still living on Hersent's milk, so while she stayed in the attic feeding them, Isengrim went hunting to feed her.

The wolves had explained that they were safe from the foxes in Silas's house, because the foxes loved rules. They would never break their rule about not going into a home without being invited – and especially not a human house.

'They learned about rules from human beings,' Isengrim said. 'Humans have rules about everything, and the foxes want to be like you.'

That was why the foxes had built their city beneath the Forest, Isengrim told Silas. Human beings had cities, so the foxes wanted one too. And a city was a place made of rules. When Isengrim and Hersent had lived there, there had been rules about when wolves had to go to work and when they had to go back to their pens, about when they were allowed to eat and what food they could have. The rules told wolves how they must speak to foxes, calling them *sir* or *ma'am* or *master* or *mistress*, and that they must not look a fox in the eye.

'The foxes get their power from their rules,' Isengrim said. 'That's why Reynard won't come in without being invited.'

They watched the pups nuzzling Hersent's belly.

'We'll stay here until they're grown,' Isengrim said. 'Until they're big and strong.'

A week passed, and when Silas stole up to the attic again he found two pups tussling on the floor. The third stuck her head around a cardboard box and watched her sisters for a minute, then pounced. Silas knew their faces by now: the largest, with her sloping eyes; the second, with her dark-tipped ears; the third, with fur paler than her sisters'.

The pups chased in a circle, nipping and squeaking. When they saw Silas they hid by the wardrobe. Then one pup came out to lick his hand. Another pup yawned, revealing the sharp clean points of her teeth.

'Soon they'll be hunting for themselves,' said Isengrim.

Just then, one of the pups made a flying leap and buried her teeth in his fur. Her sisters piled on too, and Isengrim rolled around yelping as they mobbed him.

Hersent came through the hatch. Her legs, chest and muzzle were wet, as if she had waded a shallow river. In the past few days she had begun to go out on the hunt while Isengrim took his turn staying with the pups.

The pups shoved their noses against Hersent's muzzle. She let them squeak and dance, then leaned down and brought up meat from her stomach. The pups devoured it. Silas was still not used to seeing the wolves regurgitate their food. Humans might like to carry things in their hands, Isengrim had said, but when you are a wolf the best way to bring dinner to your family is to keep it safe in your stomach.

The pups licked the floorboards clean. They began to squeak and jab at Hersent's mouth again, but she growled.

'That's all.'

'Slim pickings again?' said Isengrim, as the pups began to play.

'If we're going to bring back enough for them, we need to hunt together,' Hersent said.

'It's so soon,' Isengrim said. 'Can we leave them?'

Just then Silas gave a cry of surprise. One of the pups had leaped on him from the top of a bookcase. The other two pups ambushed him, springing from behind a crate to attack his trouser legs. He collapsed to the floor, laughing, squealing and protesting, trying to fight them off, but not really trying very hard. The pups piled on him, wagging their tails as they savaged their prey.

'You're right,' Isengrim said at last.

The wolves looked at the pile of bodies. From under the wriggling fur, a hand waved for help.

'Silas,' said Hersent, 'how do you feel about babysitting?'

Rain pattered on the attic window. The pups lay asleep in a warm pile, breathing deeply, ears and paws twitching. Their shared smell filled the attic, rich and pleasant as baking bread. Silas climbed down through the trapdoor to the landing.

Apart from Silas and the pups, the house was empty. Mum, Dad and Allie had gone into town for the afternoon, to do some shopping and see a film at the cinema. When Silas had told them he did not want to go, his parents had not been able to hide their surprise. He had never asked to do anything separately from the family before. When the other three were going somewhere together, there had never been any doubt that he would tag along. But he just didn't feel like it today, he mumbled, and besides, he had a lot of homework to finish. As Mum and Dad stared at one another, Silas thought he could follow the silent discussion that hung in the air between them. Could they trust him to stay at home by himself for the afternoon? Did he have enough common sense?

Eventually Mum nodded, and Silas thought he saw a trace of relief on Dad's face. Perhaps they would be glad to forget about him for a few hours.

Once Mum, Dad and Allie had left, Silas had gone up to the attic. He had promised Isengrim and Hersent that the pups would be fine, and the two adult wolves had gone into the Forest to hunt.

Now Silas made a sandwich and ate it at the kitchen table. Rain crawled down the window. While the pups were asleep, he thought, maybe he should do his homework.

As he got up to fetch his school bag, someone tapped on the back door.

Silas opened the door to find Reynard the fox sitting on the doormat, his front paws lined up with the word WELCOME. His fur was wet.

'Please,' he said. 'I'm not here to make trouble. I'm sure you know I would never set foot in your house without being invited.'

Silas did not close the door, but he did not open it any wider. Reynard got up and moved away from the doorstep. He sat down in the lane behind the house.

'I promise I'll come no nearer your home, if you don't want me to.'

Silas struggled to reply, but the words would not come.

'The truth is, I need to speak to you,' Reynard said. 'We got off on the wrong foot, so I've come to say I'm sorry and to ask if we can start over again.'

The fox looked down at his paws, almost as if he were shy. Under the steady rain, he was small and bedraggled, his fur clinging in damp points.

'I don't expect you to trust me at once,' he went on.

'I'm sure Isengrim and Hersent have told you lots of bad things about me. And some of them were probably true. I'm not here to argue. I only want to be honest, and the honest truth is that things have been bad between the foxes and the wolves for a long time now.'

Silas strained to speak, but the words seemed to catch in his mouth. His face was growing hot with shame under the fox's calm gaze.

'Told me ... what you did,' he said. 'Kept them prisoner. Made them work.'

'And I'm deeply sorry if that's what they believe,' Reynard said. 'Look. All I want is for wolves and foxes to live in peace. Isn't that what you want too?'

Silas nodded doubtfully.

'That's why I came to see you,' Reynard said. 'The sad truth is that the foxes and the wolves can't talk to one another. There's too much hurt and anger on both sides. But you, Silas, you can see our troubles from the outside. We can talk to you. I think you can help us get along.'

Reynard's golden eyes were wide.

'Wouldn't that be a good thing?'

'Wait,' Silas said.

The next words almost refused to come, but he took a deep breath and pushed on.

'You say ... you want to talk ... to the wolves. But they told me ... what you did. Only taught them to speak ... to make them your slaves. You were never their friend.'

Saying so much at once was exhausting, but Silas gathered his strength to force out a few more words.

'Trying ... to trick me.'

He began to close the door.

'Please!' called Reynard. 'Wait!'

He sounded so worried that Silas paused.

'No tricks,' Reynard said. 'I promise, no tricks. Let me tell you the truth.'

7

'I KNOW what they say about me,' Reynard said. 'Crafty. Cunning. Tricky. Sly.'

He sighed.

'But if you think back, Silas, you'll find I have always spoken the truth.'

He shook himself, flinging raindrops from his ears.

'I can't tell you what to think,' he said. 'I wouldn't try. But perhaps you'll let me tell you a story.'

The wide golden eyes gazed up, as if to ask what harm that could do.

'It was the winter after Isengrim and Hersent ran away,' Reynard said. 'That was a hard season in the Forest. Food was scarce and storms were fierce, and we were worried for the wolves, lost out there in the wilderness. I was the most worried of all. They were my responsibility and I couldn't forget them. I went searching all over the Forest.

'It took me all winter, but at last I found a trail which led me somewhere I had not expected. I had thought to find the wolves hiding in a lonely part of the Forest, but I was wrong. They had gone to the places where the humans lived.

'I followed the wolves' traces through that human city,' Reynard said. 'Eventually I tracked them to a farm. Actually, it wasn't a real farm: it was a play-farm, a pretend place, one of those charming inventions that only humans could come up with. It was a children's farm, the kind where they keep a few animals for the young humans to visit, to stroke them and start learning about them. Perhaps you've been to a place like that yourself.'

Reynard paused and gazed up through the falling rain.

'Understand me, Silas,' he said. 'I am telling you this story for a reason. I am telling you how I came to learn the nature of wolves.

'So. A farm for children to visit and make friends with the adorable creatures. This one had ducks, rabbits, sheep, goats, little pigs, a Shetland pony. It was midnight when I arrived there and spotted the wolves slinking around the fence. I could smell all the animals asleep inside. I could smell the hunger of the wolves.

'Remember, I was alone. I was one small fox. I could do nothing to stop what was about to happen. I could only watch as they tore through the gates and attacked the farm, smashing the pens and coops to get at the animals inside.

'I won't describe what I saw that night. I'll just say that no animal escaped. When the wolves had finished, they were red with blood from their muzzles to their tails, and the farm was a slaughterhouse.

'Now, wolves kill to eat. We know this. But these wolves must have killed ten times as much as they could eat between them that night. I couldn't understand it. Killing not for food, but because they love to kill.'

Silas swallowed. His throat was dry.

'Not ... true,' he croaked.

'Tell yourself that if you like,' Reynard said. 'But wolves kill for the sake of killing. Don't take my word for it. Use the power you humans have at your fingertips. Go to your computer and type in the word *wolves*. Then type *surplus killing*. In five minutes you'll understand what I'm talking about. You'll learn that, given the chance, wolves will kill and kill and kill. It's sometimes called henhouse syndrome, this love of murder. You might read that it's not their fault: that they are bred to hunt where prey is scarce, and that their instincts get confused when they find too many victims. As if we can't expect wolves to control themselves when they've tasted blood.

'I don't know about that,' Reynard said. 'All I know is that, whatever the cause, I don't feel safe with predators who can kill in that way.'

He blinked away the rain.

'I'm not trying to scare you, Silas. I'm simply raising a question. Do you think that creatures like this, creatures who kill for no reason you or I can understand, should be on the loose in the civilised world?'

Silas wanted to speak, but the words had given up on him again.

'There's never only one side to a story,' Reynard said. 'What the wolves have told you about the foxes is true. We taught them to speak and brought them to live in our city. But believe me when I tell you our intentions were good. Think of how it was for us. How were we to know they couldn't cope with our gifts? Perhaps we were reckless. Perhaps we should never have offered the wolves a better way of life. But we only wanted to help them.'

Reynard sighed again.

'They're out hunting now, aren't they?' he said. 'But if they come back with empty bellies, how long will those pups go hungry before Isengrim starts to look at you in a different way? Before he starts thinking what a fine meal you'd make?'

Silas shook his head.

'Are you sure?' Reynard said. 'Can you really tell me you've never felt the slightest bit unsafe with the wolves?'

Silas opened his mouth to reply. But then he remembered the fright he had got when he first met Isengrim on the cycle path. He remembered the wolf crashing into the shed at school, and he remembered him regurgitating a mess of flesh for Hersent to eat. He thought of the bone-cracking jaw strength that was already there, barely checked, in the play-bites of the pups. He thought of dozens of times when the wolves had seemed like strange and dangerous creatures.

'Look,' said Reynard, 'I don't blame anyone for being the way nature made them. I'm a predator myself. I have no quarrel with animals who hunt for their dinners. But unlike the wolves, we foxes have our animal instincts under control. We learned that from you, Silas: from human beings. We taught the wolves to speak, but the words came from you in the first place.

'Foxes and humans are on the same side, because we know that rules matter. *Words* matter. They let us agree on what is right and what is wrong. That's what makes us different from the wolves and from all the other animals of the Forest. Words make rules, and rules make us better. They protect the weak and discipline the strong, and they make us work together for the good of us all.

'And all I want now is for us to sit down together – fox, wolf and human – and see if we can't find a better way for them to live with us.'

Reynard was soaked through. With his fur clinging, he looked small and frail.

'That's all I have to say,' he said. 'Maybe you'll want to discuss it with your wolves, when they get back from the hunt. So I'll be going.'

He got up.

'Wait,' Silas said.

Reynard looked around. Silas fought to get the next words out.

'You're having some trouble there,' Reynard said. 'Maybe I can help. Maybe what you want to say is that there can't be any harm in talking about this a little more. Is that right?'

Silas nodded.

'Maybe you want to say that I shouldn't leave quite yet? That the wolves will be back soon, and then we can work it all out?'

Silas hesitated. Then he nodded again. The conversation had drained him as if he had just run a race. He only wanted to go back inside the house and recover, but Reynard was gazing up at him, the golden eyes so large and steady and expectant that Silas felt he could not move. He could not think of anything to do except what he knew the fox was waiting for.

'Come in,' he said.

Foxes do not smile. But the way that Reynard's eyes changed, sharpening to a look of triumph, told Silas that if the fox could smile he would have been smiling a very toothy smile indeed.

'I thought you'd never ask.'

All at once they appeared. Scores of foxes; hundreds of foxes; more foxes than Silas had ever seen or imagined. They came fast, in silence, ignoring him as they flooded into the house. They surged through the back hall and into the kitchen, pawing open cupboard doors and scattering what was inside. They ransacked the living room. Glass broke. Fabric ripped. Claws tore the carpet.

Silas stood by uselessly as foxes swarmed up the stairs towards the attic. He did not know what to do. The pups squeaked as they were dragged down the stairs, each held at the scruff of the neck by one of three big rust-red foxes. All the foxes retreated through the kitchen and the hall, out of the back door and into the lane. Silas trailed after them in a daze.

Reynard was there, surrounded by his own kind. Saffron stood beside him, and at the sight of the wolf pups she showed her teeth.

'You humans are odd about wolves,' Reynard said. 'You're so frightened of them, but you've hurt them far more than they could ever hurt you. Do you know there have been times when your species has declared war on the wolf? Your governments pay money for their corpses. You kill them for sport. You break their bones with your traps and blow their brains out with your guns. You feed them poison so whole packs die in agony. You chase them with helicopters until they drop dead from exhaustion, and you think it's fun. And all the time you're telling one another stories about what savage beasts they are. I never could work out why it was so important for humans to wipe wolves from the face of the world.'

Silas made the dumb noises that he made when he wanted to speak but the words would not come.

'Time to go,' Reynard said. 'It's been a pleasure.'

The wolf pups were not much smaller than the foxes holding them, but the foxes were skilful and cruel, and the pups could not break free. They squirmed and mewled.

Then, from the far end of the lane, their cries were answered. The wolves came running for their pups, their eyes wild and teeth bared, saliva flying. The wolves' fur was stained pink, streaked and darkening to bloody muzzles. Their hunt had gone well, Silas thought, marvelling at how slowly this chaos was passing.

The foxes were slipping through a cast-iron gate that closed off the lane's other end. The first of the three rusty foxes pushed the first of the pups between the bars.

As the wolves charged past Silas, Isengrim's shoulder knocked him against the wall.

The iron gate was heavy. It was chained and padlocked and bolted into the brick. As the wolves closed the distance, the second and third pups were pushed between the bars. The gaps were big enough for foxes and wolf pups to pass, but not for adult wolves. As the last of the foxes darted through the gate, Hersent caught up with them and slammed into the bars.

The iron rang as she attacked it. She forced her head through, but her pups were out of reach. She could only snap and snarl as the foxes dragged them away.

One fox did not disappear with the rest. It was Saffron. She trotted back towards the gate and stood just beyond the range of Hersent's jaws. She watched the wolf curiously, unfazed by the snarls and the clanging of the gate.

Saffron lunged and sunk her teeth into Hersent's face. There was a horrible shriek. The fox hung on as the wolf flailed. Then she fell back, licking blood from her chops, and followed after the other foxes.

The clanging ceased. Hersent collapsed to the ground and lay still. Isengrim stood, bloody-headed, at the gate where his pups had disappeared.

He howled.

———•———

Silas drifted from room to room, trying to start clearing up the mess. He righted a fallen lamp. He scrubbed with a tissue at the paw marks printed across a sofa cushion, then turned the cushion over and put it back in its place. These small gestures were no use at all. The house was wrecked: the floors were covered in broken glass and pages from books; pictures had been torn from the walls and curtains from their rails. In the living room, Mum's favourite armchair had been ripped open, and the television had been knocked to the floor. Scrapes and slashes of claws and teeth were all around, and a rank smell of foxes hung in the air.

He did not know where the wolves had gone. After the foxes escaped, Isengrim had helped Hersent free of the gate, and the wolves had retreated into a clump of bushes at the far side of the lane. Silas hoped they had left him for good. Now that the wolves knew what a mistake it had been to place their trust in a fool, a weakling, a coward like him, he hoped they would disappear into the Forest so he would never have to be reminded of the disaster he had brought them.

He wiped streaks of mud from the hall skirting boards, but this only revealed the deep gouges that had been inflicted on the paint and the wood. The foxes had attacked the house with such savage glee. Either they must love destruction for its own sake, Silas thought, or they must truly hate human beings and our houses.

There was no way he could clean up the mess and fix everything that was broken before his family got home. In a few hours they would come back and discover the wreck, and he did not know what would happen after that. He could not even imagine how upset and angry they would be.

Then he heard a voice.

'Silas.'

Isengrim was standing in the hall.

'Please, come with me.'

———◆———

A black shape was perched on the fence behind the house, huddled against the rain. Corax the raven cocked her head. Her eye was a bead of black ink. To Silas it seemed full of scorn. The raven made a sound like knocking on wood: *Toc-toc-toc.* Then she opened her wings and was gone, flapping into the heavy sky.

Hersent was lying under the bushes by the lane, her side hitching fast with her breathing. One side of her face was ragged and swollen, and where her eye belonged there was a bloody wound. Her other eye was open, but it stared at nothing.

Isengrim licked at her muzzle.

'She can't wake up,' he said.

Hersent's whole body twitched. Then she was still again, except for the working of her lungs. Silas had a pain in his stomach. He wanted to ask what was going to happen to the pups, but he knew that trying to speak now would be useless.

'Reynard does not want dead wolves,' Isengrim said. 'He wants wolves tamed and broken. He wants to own them.'

Silas tried to say something, not knowing what, but the wolf growled.

'If we're to get them back, we must make Hersent well,' Isengrim said.

Shivers were running through the mother wolf. Silas wondered if she was dreaming.

'When you were fox-bitten, we healed you with a kind of earth,' Isengrim said. 'A special clay with the virtue to mend a wound like this.'

'Hersent said you gave me your last piece.'

'So now we must fetch more,' Isengrim said. 'The clay is found in only one place. It is not easy to reach, but I know the way. We leave at once.'

It took Silas a few moments to understand what the wolf meant: that he was supposed to go too. It made no sense, he thought. Isengrim did not need him. He only got things wrong and made things worse. He shook his head.

Isengrim growled.

'If you choose not to help us, so be it,' he said. 'I shall wish you well and you will not see us any more.'

The wolf came closer.

'Perhaps that would be better for you. Perhaps there is nothing for you to gain by joining us in what comes next. So leave us for your own sake. But not for ours.'

He looked at his injured mate, then at Silas.

'Because we need you.'

8

IT WAS evening when they reached the cave.

Isengrim had a nylon rope looped around his neck. He was hauling the plastic toboggan that Silas had found in the garage at home. They had made the unconscious Hersent as comfortable on it as they could. Isengrim had told Silas to bring what a human needed for a journey, so Silas had packed a satchel with a bottle of water, a blanket, a packet of chocolate biscuits and some dried fruit. He had put on a fleece sweater and his waterproof jacket. On Isengrim's advice, he had also taken an electric torch and the long coil of narrow white rope that had been hanging near the toboggan in the garage. He had tried to write a note to leave on the kitchen table for his family to find when they got home, but he did not know how to explain what had happened or where he was going. Maybe it was better to leave without saying anything at all.

The journey seemed different from their other travels through the Forest. Their surroundings changed faster than Silas could understand. They were in damp, warm woodland, their feet squelching, but then they came to a ridge scoured by bone-chilling wind and saw distant mountains as sharp and lucent as chunks of broken glass. A gully led them into a place where the wind grew warm and gusty and blew sheets of newspaper around in a smell of fried food and old vegetable peelings. They were in a back street of a city, but right away Isengrim led him through an underpass and the city noise that roared overhead became the noise of wind in the branches of gigantic trees. Silas clambered over roots thicker than his own body and followed the wolf among trunks as broad as houses.

Now, as they stood in front of the cave, he felt they had come much further than they should have been able to travel in the few hours they had been walking. The hill bulked above them like the silhouette of some giant slumbering creature. The sky behind was bright with evening light, but down here they were in shadow.

They eased Hersent off the toboggan, into the shelter of some thorny bushes with tiny white flowers. In the failing light the side of her face was a dark mass. Silas did not look closely. He did not want to see how bad the injury was, but he caught a foul smell: a stink that should not be able to come from any healthy creature, like the smell that filled the bathroom when the toilet pipes were blocked.

'Rest and eat,' said Isengrim. 'Don't be long.'

Silas swigged water and chewed biscuits and dried apricots. The hill was huge above him, but more enormous still was the silence of the evening. Forest and sky were filled with a silence like nothing Silas had ever heard: peacefulness so perfect that it tolled like a bell. The cave mouth resembled a half-open door. A slab of stone stood away from the rock face, leaving a gap of darkness.

'Now,' said Isengrim.

Silas got up. *OK*, he thought, *what do I do?*

As they travelled here, the wolf had explained that Silas would have to work out for himself how to get safely into the cave. It was a puzzle, and solving puzzles was for humans, not for wolves. It was humans who could go into places where they had never been meant to go, humans who came up with ideas and inventions, tools and tricks and clever plans. That, Isengrim said, was how Silas could help the wolves.

He tried to think. A white-flowered bush was growing in front of the cave mouth. He emptied out his satchel on the ground, picked up the coil of rope and tied one end to the root of the bush. He put the satchel strap across his shoulder and clicked the torch on, throwing a patch of yellow light over the rocks.

Isengrim touched his nose to the nose of his mate. When he looked up at Silas, the wolf's eyes were full of green reflections.

Silas went into the cave.

The torch lit a tunnel in the rock. Stooping so as not to bump his head, he paid out the white cord and moved towards the darkness beyond the torchlight. Sometimes he had to duck, and sometimes he had to squeeze, but the passage into the hill was easy enough. He tried not to think of the weight of earth and stone above him, or the darkness that would swallow him if the torch failed.

Then the passage ended in a wall. Playing the beam over the uneven rock, he saw a flat slot between two slabs. He eased his head and shoulders into the crack and found himself sandwiched between two surfaces of rock, a few inches apart, sloping downwards as he crawled.

The space between the slabs tightened, and he realised his head was jammed. It was like being gripped between two giant teeth. His heart beat hard. He could not go back or go on. An awful picture formed in his mind of a lightless depth of granite, as vast as an ocean, and at the very bottom a speck that was Silas himself, a wriggling insect clamped in the jaw of the mountain. He shut his eyes. The stone was cold and hard and unyielding, and even the smallest movement tore at the skin of his temples. Breathing slow and deep, trying not to panic, he made cautious experiments and found that he could, with care, withdraw from the grip of the rock. He eased his head free and kept crawling. The torchlight spilled ahead. The empty satchel dragged along beside him. The cord unwound.

At last he reached forward and touched nothing. The lower surface of the shaft ended in a shelf. The torch showed a rock floor, a metre and a half below, so he pulled himself over the edge and found he could stand upright again.

He was in a cavern.

The light slid across arches and ridges of rock, dissolving into dark. He pointed the torch upwards and a cluster of stalactites sprouted from the darkness, hanging like pale, knobbly strings from the cave roof. On the floor below them, stalagmites bulged like mushrooms. Silas shivered. Down here the air was damp and earthy, and the chill was creeping into his bones.

A drop of water plopped and echoed.

He took a step forwards, his breath turning to fog in the torchlight. The floor of the chamber had the same pale gleam as the stalactites. It felt hard and a little slippery. His foot knocked against something and he swung the beam down. The skull of a horned animal was half buried in the floor.

He had never known such darkness. It pressed on him with all the weight of the mountain. Down here, the light of the torch seemed so small and weak that he felt the dark itself might begin to laugh.

Silence.

Chime of water.

Silence.

Isengrim had told him that he had to cross to the other side of the chamber. He trod slowly, running the torchlight over the rock. He was halfway across when he found that he was holding the end of the white cord. He looked back at the line sagging into the dark. He could not get any further without letting it go; but that would mean letting go of the only sure way of returning to the surface.

Unless he was going to go back to the wolves empty-handed, he had no choice. He looked around, trying to remember exactly where he was standing. He laid the cord on the floor and took another step.

Then his heart lurched, and the light of the torch bounced madly around the chamber. At the edge of his vision, something had moved. He held his breath, his blood beating in his ears, waiting for some pale and faceless monster of the cave to spring at him from the dark.

He waited. There was only silence and echoing water. He swung the torch back to the place where he had seen the movement. On a bulging rock wall, the light revealed a drawing. A picture of a deer. The lines had been carved into the rock and coloured with dark pigments. The deer was running. The drawing had a fluency which made it seem to move as the light slid across. The animal's eye was no more than a dark dot, but it was looking at him.

The torchlight slipped along the wall, and more animals came alive. Horses, elk, reindeer, bison, cows and bulls, even rhinoceros and elephants. Lions, bears and wolves. All of them running, leaping, striding or rearing, and all fixing him with their black-spot eyes. The animals ran across the walls of the chamber, into the darkness. As he stared at them, an urge came over him, and after a minute he obeyed it.

He turned off his torch.

At the instant he did so, it was as if there had never been any light. Not down here, not anywhere in the universe. He could not tell if he was standing or falling, awake or asleep. He was barely here at all. All there was of him, in this dark, was a voice saying to itself: *What if I drop the torch now? What if I throw it away and hear it smash on the rocks?*

He clicked the switch and the light came back. For the rest of his life he would wonder why he had turned it off.

Cross the great chamber, Isengrim had told him. *There are many passages beyond, and you must choose the right one. Look for a blue column.*

He swung the torch. He had thought the column would be easy to spot. He had imagined a smooth, vertical, brightly coloured pillar, but there was nothing like that here. All he could see was a jumble of rocks. He told himself to take his time and look more carefully. He stilled the beam and let it move steadily across the cave.

And he saw it. A stalactite and a stalagmite had joined to make a spindly column. The slick mineral surface gleamed with a faint blue tint. Beyond, an opening between two sheets of rock was large enough to let him through.

You will find the clay under your feet, Isengrim had said. And now, as he moved into the narrower chamber, the texture underfoot softened. He shone the torch down. The floor was a blue-black substance in which a few bright flecks glittered. He lifted a foot and saw the print of his trainer.

You will know the place when you see the footprints, Isengrim had said. *Down there, traces are not worn away by time. Tracks in clay will last for a thousand lifetimes, as fresh as the day they were made.*

He took another step on the clay. His trainer lifted with a faint sucking sound. Then he saw them. A short way to his left, a trail of prints in the clay led on into the dark.

This was it, then. He squatted, placing the torch on the ground, and pressed his fingers into the clay. He dug out a double handful and stowed in in his satchel.

Now
that he had
what he had
come for, Silas felt
more than ever the weight
of rock and darkness beneath which
he was buried. It was time to leave, but he
did not retrace his steps at once. Instead he
thought of what Isengrim had said: *Look for the footprints.*

Torchlight showed the prints in the clay. There were
two sets of tracks walking side by side, unknowably long
ago. One trail was a large animal with clawed, doglike
pads. The other was a human being. Not a full-grown one:
the bare feet that made the prints had been a little smaller
than his own.

He followed the tracks down the narrow chamber,
making his own prints alongside. At last the tracks ended
at a wall of rock. He was disappointed to find nothing
more. No clue to the fate of those who had once
walked on this clay, no destination at the end of
the trail.

Then the torchlight strayed up the rock's surface, so that movement seemed to course through the figures that were drawn there, marked into the cave wall with a few skilful lines.

Two figures running side by side, as companions. One a wolf. The other a human child.

———•———

The sky was frosted with stars. Silas had never seen such a clear night, or such a blaze of starlight across the darkness. When he looked into the darker parts of the sky, lesser stars became visible there too, growing brighter as he stared. And if he looked again into the darkness beyond, then yet fainter stars would show. He could keep gazing into the sky forever, further and deeper, and never cease to find starlight.

He shivered in his blanket and edged closer to Isengrim.

Hersent was still unconscious, but her sleep was no longer feverish. She breathed deeply and easily. The side of her face was masked with the blue-black clay, which Isengrim had tongued on the wound. Her whines and tremors had ceased, and since then she had not stirred from her sleep.

They looked at the stars.

Silas's hands were tingling. He could still feel the cold weight of the clay he had carried. He opened his hands. They were blue-black in the darkness, and in his palms he saw tiny flecks of brightness twinkling.

Isengrim spoke in a slow murmur, quiet as the night.

'Once, when the Forest was young, the foxes gave language to the wolves. The wolves learned to name the Forest around us, rock and tree and pack and prey. But we also learned to name things inside us. We found that we had dreams and stories. We gave names to things that we had never seen or heard or touched, but that we knew in ourselves to be true.

'We had a name for a certain human child. This was the child who would walk side by side with the wolves and would know our silence and speak for us. The child would be our voice, so that we would not need to speak any longer. So that we could live as wolves ought to live. Free from words.'

Silas eased himself onto the ground against Isengrim's side. His eyes began to close, and the last thing he heard before he slept was the murmur of the wolf, saying: 'The name for that child was Wolfstongue.'

Silas dreamed.

He was clay, deep down in the ground. But the dream of life was so strong in the clay that it shaped itself into a new form. It climbed through the darkness and pulled itself to the surface in the shape of a boy. The boy began to run. Wolves ran beside him, and the boy felt words come to his tongue. As he ran, he sang out the words. He told a story of how he and the wolves were the same clay. And when all the words were gone, the boy shaped himself into a new form. He ran faster and faster, on his four strong paws, and vanished into the Forest with the rest of the wolves.

———•———

Dawn light spread down the face of the cave hill, colouring rocks and shrubs, as Silas woke.

The clay on Hersent's face had dried to a pale crust. Isengrim licked until her face was clean. She got to her feet, unsteadily at first, and paced around the clearing. She shook her head as if to rid herself of sleep. Her right eye was lively and clear, but the left was sealed over for good. A white scar ran from her eyebrow to her lip.

Isengrim whined and rubbed his nose into the fur at her throat.

The sky behind the hill was clear and pale, and a speck was drifting in the haze. It might have been nothing, a fault in Silas's vision, but it did not disappear. It grew steady and solid, and descended, flapping dark wings.

A harsh sound echoed off the hill – *kraa kraa* – and Corax the raven landed in a tree.

'You have news?' Isengrim said.

'*Kraa.*' The raven pecked at something on the branch. 'Found them. Flew high, kept out of sight, tracked them. They went deep into the Forest.'

The raven circled the clearing and touched down by Silas and the wolves. She seemed about to speak, then stopped and combed at the underside of her wing with the tip of her beak.

'Say it,' Isengrim said.

'They went there,' she said. 'They took the pups through the gate.'

The wolves looked grim.

'What is it?' Silas asked.

'They've taken them into the Earth,' said Isengrim. 'The pups are in the underground city of the foxes.'

9

THE WOLVES bounded through the trees, Silas riding on Isengrim's back.

'The city of Earth is the most dangerous place in the Forest, for wolves,' Isengrim said. 'In there, Reynard rules. Even if we could break in without being caught, finding the pups would be hard enough, and getting them out would be almost impossible.'

'What are you going to do?' Silas asked, only noticing once the words were out how easily they had come. Despite everything, he could still talk better when it was just him and the wolves.

Hersent growled.

'We're going to break into the city,' she said. 'We're going to find the pups. And we're going to get them out.'

The wolves slowed as they trotted up a slope. The ground had been mulchy forest floor, strewn with leaf litter and sprouting swathes of bracken, but now it was a neglected cement path. They pushed through a thicket and between two panels of a worn-out wooden fence. They were at the bottom of an overgrown garden, facing the rear of a semi-detached house.

'Why are we here?'

'We've come for help,' Isengrim said.

A cat strolled down the garden towards them. It was Tybalt.

'Well, well,' he said, once the wolves had explained why they had come. 'That's too bad about the pups. Sneaking into the fox city is a crazy idea, obviously. Two great big wolves like you have no chance of getting in unnoticed. You need someone who can be invisible, someone who can jump and climb and sneak and slip through gaps that are barely there at all. So I can see why you came to me. I'm the best.'

He was smiling neatly behind his whiskers, as usual.

'What I don't quite get is this. What are you going to give me in return? If I'm not mistaken, you're trying to engage my services, and I expect to be paid.'

The wolves looked at one another.

'We can't pay you,' Hersent said. 'We have nothing to give.'

'What about him?' Tybalt said, seeming to notice Silas

for the first time. Silas wondered what sort of payment a cat would want.

'I could ... get you some tins of cat food?'

Tybalt hissed.

'I shall ignore that,' he said. 'Let me explain something. I do exactly as I like. One day I might hunt mice and voles in the nature reserve. The next I might go far into the Forest and have an exotic endangered songbird for my lunch. Then another day I might drop into the Watson family down the street. They call me Tom and argue over who gets to have me sleep on their bed. They truly believe I belong to them. Or I might visit the delightful Miss Damson and her flatmates, who like to give me saucers of double cream and scratch my tummy while I lounge on their laps. They think my name is Mack. Or else I might come here, where Mrs Chester feeds me fresh salmon straight from the fishmonger.

'I do as I like, and I live like a king, and you'll forgive me if I'm not terribly impressed by your invitation to risk my neck for a few tins of cat food.'

Silas's cheeks were growing warm. He did not know what to say.

The back window of the house opened, and they heard the *ting-ting-ting* of a fork tapped against a saucer. Next came a high, quavering voice: 'Oh, Mr Snooky-Buttercups! Come along, you naughty pussy! Your din-dins is ready!'

Tybalt lashed his tail.

85

'The old lady calls me Mr Snooky-Buttercups,' he muttered. 'I don't really know why.'

'Enough of this,' Isengrim said. 'We came because we thought you'd want to help us. You helped thwart the foxes before, when they had Silas. And besides, you have your own reasons to hate them.'

At that, the stump of Tybalt's torn ear twitched. But then he laughed.

'You're quite wrong, my dear wolves. I have no feelings about the foxes one way or the other, because nothing they do can possibly make a difference to me. I say, let them build cities under the Forest if they must. Let them kidnap younglings if they like. It doesn't matter to Tybalt. I helped you rescue the boy because I was bored. If I'd been in another mood that day, I wouldn't have bothered.'

Hersent snarled.

'We're wasting time,' she said.

The *ting-ting-ting* of fork on saucer rang out from the house as the wolves turned away.

'Din-dins!' sang the quavering voice.

'You know what?' Tybalt said. 'I do fancy a little caper. Just for the fun of it, I'll come with you.'

He strolled past Silas towards the gap in the fence.

'Make sure it's *nice* cat food,' he said.

———————•◆•———————

They plunged through the Forest. As the wolves ran, Silas glimpsed Tybalt keeping up with them, darting across open ground, leaping between branches. They followed a river upstream in a valley whose sides were so steep that light filtered down green and dim, and huge ferns hung in their path.

They came to a dreary place where dry trunks stuck out from a barren slope. Human rubbish lay scattered on the ground: cans and bottles, plastic bags, a cracked car tyre. Hundreds of winged insects danced on the surface of a stagnant pool. Beside the pool stood a huge brown boulder.

But as they got closer, Silas saw it was not a boulder. It could not be, because it was covered in brown fur, and it moved, turning to unfold two front legs as thick as tree trunks and plant two paws as big as car tyres on the ground. The animal's face was a great disc of brown fur, with a wet black nose and toffee-coloured eyes.

'Hello, Bruno,' Isengrim said.

The bear blinked slowly.

'It's been a long time,' he said at last.

'We need your help,' said Hersent.

While the wolves spoke with the bear, Silas kept his distance, unsettled by the sheer size of the creature in front of him. Tybalt the cat sat down nearby and licked the back of his paw with a clean pink tongue.

'Quite the specimen, isn't he?'

'How ...?' Silas began. He could not get the rest of the question out.

'How indeed,' Tybalt said, and chuckled. 'How is he so big? How is he here at all, come to that, when his kind died out in this part of the world some time during the last ice age?'

Silas nodded, mystified.

'Think of it like this,' said the cat. 'The Forest goes everywhere. And contrary to what your species tends to believe, things often look bigger when they're further away.'

Silas had no idea what Tybalt was talking about, but the cat did not seem inclined to explain further.

'We need you to help us get the pups back,' Isengrim was saying to the bear. 'We need your strength.'

Bruno the bear straightened up. He drew his huge mass together until he towered over the wolves, the cat and the boy. He gazed down at them like a totem. Then, very slowly, he sighed and slumped.

'I have no strength,' he said. 'I can barely lift my own weight.'

He raised a paw and let it thump into the dust.

'But you were so strong when you worked for the foxes,' Isengrim said. 'When we built their Great Hall, I saw you lift stones with one paw that no other animal could have moved an inch.'

'They used up my strength,' Bruno said. 'They wore me out, and when I was no more use they drove me away. They said that if I showed my face again they would tear me to pieces.'

'Then make them pay,' Hersent said. 'Come back to the Earth with us and show the foxes what a mistake it was to treat you that way.'

Bruno shook his head.

'I can't go back there,' he said. 'They took my courage from me, as well as my strength.'

Stiffly and painfully, the bear got up. He turned his hindquarters on them and began to lumber into the trees, between the spills of rubbish.

'Bruno!' Isengrim called, but the bear did not look around. He carried on walking.

'You have my answer, wolf.'

———•———

An hour later they had left the barren place behind. They were crossing a shallow bowl of red-brown moorland, one side of which sloped up to a long, curving scarp of blocky gritstone, when a *kraa kraa* made them look around.

Corax the raven was perched on a rock.

'Ah, my feathery pal's here,' Tybalt said. 'Still not been eaten, I see. Want me to help you out with that?'

'No,' Corax said. 'And I notice you talk about catching birds a lot more than you actually do it.'

Tybalt laughed. 'Would you listen to her! Absurd!' He chuckled. 'Absurd.'

'I've brought one more,' Corax told the wolves. She glanced down behind the rock. 'Come on, Todd. Say hello.'

An animal slunk into the open. At the sight of it, the wolves snarled. It was a fox. Silas's heart beat faster, but the new arrival did not look threatening. He cowered from the wolves as if all he wanted was to run away.

Corax flapped her wings and cawed.

'Let's stay calm,' she said. 'We're all on the same side.'

'I doubt that,' Isengrim said. The fox flinched.

'Todd wants to help,' Corax said. 'He's taken a risk by coming here. He can tell us what's going on in the city.'

'Why should we believe anything he says?' Isengrim said.

'Go ahead, Todd,' said Corax. 'You can explain.'

Todd was a scruffy animal. His whiskers looked as if he had slept on them at a funny angle. He glanced around nervously.

'I'm just an ordinary fox,' he said. 'I work in the Citadel, but I'm nobody special. I just carry messages.' He swallowed. 'I mean, I did until today.'

'Get to the point,' Hersent said.

'Right. Well, I'm not important, but I hear the rumours that go around. Yesterday I started hearing about the wolf pups. I heard they'd been captured. I felt I had to find out more. So I sneaked into a part of the Citadel where I'm not meant to go, and I overheard two of the guard-foxes talking. They were Brother Reynard's elite guards: the same ones who snatched the pups. That's what they were saying, anyway. They said the pups are alive and well, but they're in the deepest, best-protected place in the city.'

'The Keep,' said Isengrim.

The fox nodded. 'That's what I heard.'

'Why would you want to help us?' Hersent said.

Todd looked unhappy.

'Things aren't going well in the Earth,' he said. 'A lot of foxes are worried. They say the city was meant to bring a better life for every fox. But since the wolves disappeared, all the work they used to do has to be done by foxes instead. Cleaning the tunnels, bringing in supplies, digging and building, hauling out the rubbish and the dirt, running the machinery. It turns out that a city needs a lot of hard, dirty work to keep it going. The foxes didn't think they'd be the ones having to do it.

'And while ordinary foxes are doing those jobs, Brother Reynard and the other important foxes are living the high life, down there in the Lower City. That's what a lot of foxes are saying. They say life in the city isn't fair, and they're getting angry about it. Some are saying Reynard shouldn't be our leader.'

Todd's eyes flicked from side to side, as if he were afraid someone else might be listening.

'The city feels dangerous. Some are saying Saffron would be a better leader, that she'd be strong and bold and she'd sort out all our problems. Lots of foxes think it's only a matter of time until she makes her move against Reynard. They say it's time to pick sides. That there's going to be a big fight.'

'And what do you think?' Isengrim asked.

'I don't know. Life isn't good with Reynard in charge, but I can't see how Saffron would be any better. We need something else. Something different.'

'All right,' Isengrim said. 'You don't like the way things are going in your city. But why do you want to help us get our pups back?'

'Don't you see? That's the reason I decided. It was when I heard those guard-foxes talking about the plans Reynard has for your pups. When I heard, I knew I couldn't be part of the city of Earth any longer. So I sneaked out and came looking for you, and the raven found me.'

'What do you mean, plans?' said Hersent. Her voice was low and dangerous.

'Those wolf pups aren't just trophies for Brother Reynard. They're his whole solution. They're the way he's going to make himself a popular leader again. He's going to use them to make sure that soon no fox will have to do work that foxes shouldn't have to do.'

Todd cringed, as if he feared what the wolves might do to him. He swallowed hard and took a deep breath.

'Those wolf pups,' Todd said, 'are going to be the first of a new race of slaves.'

10

THE PARTY travelled through the Forest: Silas and the wolves, with Todd hurrying behind and Tybalt patrolling ahead. Corax was a dark speck sailing above, watching for surprises. They were not moving fast. As they came close to the city of the foxes, it was more important to be cautious.

Towards the middle of the day they rested. Branches scattered sunlight across the bodies of the animals as they drank from a stream. Silas filled his water bottle before sitting down to finish off the biscuits and dried fruit in his satchel. He leaned against the rugged bark of a tree that reached out to cast its shade on a place where the water ran down a rocky course and plunged into a pool, the flow singing a continuous chord. Further off, galleries of green light hung behind the trunks.

Tybalt stared at the undergrowth, then pounced, vanishing for a moment to reappear with something in his jaws: something that had been a small, furry creature and was now a bloody rag. He gnawed at his prize.

'Don't get me wrong,' he said to Silas, licking his face clean. 'Normally I get a lot more fun out of a vole before I finish it off. But we're in a hurry.'

The wolves had walked on a little further and were talking intently. It looked as though they were having an argument. They kept glancing deeper into the woods, into a shadowed glade where, Silas now saw, the ruins of buildings lay among the trees: a broken archway wrapped in creepers, a crumbling wall, a row of broad stone pillars worn down to stubs.

Silas got up, stretched his legs and wandered towards the wolves. He hung back behind a shaggy branch. They were too busy arguing to notice him, but he could hear their voices.

'He's no use to us,' Hersent was saying. 'He'll put us in more danger.'

'He can do what we can't,' Isengrim said. 'He speaks against the foxes, turns their words against them. He's our Wolfstongue.'

Hersent snarled.

'Wolfstongue,' she said. 'A foolish story. As if we need help from human beings! He was no help when they came for our pups. And now we need to act like wolves. Real wolves, who don't place their trust in humans.'

A twig crunched under Silas's shoe, and both wolves looked up, Isengrim flattening his ears against his head, Hersent baring her teeth.

'Let ...' Silas said. He had to stop and try again. 'Let me ...'

Hersent stalked towards him, staring with one clear grey eye and one white scar where an eye had been.

'I know why you gave up my pups,' she said. 'I know how the fox made you frightened. He convinced you the stories you humans tell about wolves are true. That we're evil, bloodthirsty beasts. I saw how you looked at us when we came back from the hunt. You saw us the way Reynard had taught you to see. You saw killers.'

'But you ...' Silas stammered. 'The blood. You did kill something.'

'We killed, yes. But you have no idea what that means.'

Silas gripped the branch as if it might offer some protection. With Hersent's eye fixed on him, he felt he could not move.

'While you were letting the fox tell you stories, we were hunting red deer,' she said. 'We tracked them through woodland. We stalked around the edges of the herd. We took plenty of time. We let the deer see we were there. That's how it is when we hunt. The prey know us, and they know why we come. We waited, and at last one of the deer came towards us. She looked into our eyes. She made sure we understood what we had to do. When she knew we were ready, she began to run, and we began to chase her.

'We didn't choose the deer we killed. She chose us for her death.'

The wolf growled.

'Humans think everything is winning or losing,' she said. 'But the hunt isn't like that. We didn't win, and the deer we killed did not lose. She gave her life and we took it, but it was a gift. The wolves gained something but so did the deer. What happens between wolves and our prey is not what you mean by killing. It's not savagery or murder. It's a pact.'

Silas shook his head, trying to understand.

'You don't get it,' Hersent said. 'And you never will, because you're a human. Which is why you have no business travelling any further with us.'

Silas looked to Isengrim, but the great grey wolf was silent.

Hersent came closer. Silas thought of the times when people at school made fun of him, and he felt so angry that he wanted to hurt someone or break something. Once he had kicked a bench in the playground and given himself a purple toenail. The way he had felt at those times was the way Hersent looked now. Full of anger that had nowhere to go.

Silas could not follow what happened next. One moment he was face to face with the wolf, catching the stink of blood on her breath and seeing her face transformed by rage, the muzzle corrugated, black lips drawn back to expose the fangs. The next moment he was running through the trees, stumbling, slipping on moss, thinking of nothing but the need to get away from the beast behind him. He could see nothing but the foliage that battered his face, and all he could hear was his own breath pounding in and out.

At last he could not run any further. He leaned on his knees, gulping air, and waited for his heart to slow down. He could no longer tell which way he had come. Narrow grey-green trunks snaked away on all sides. He turned in a circle, disoriented.

'Silas.'

He started; he looked around. Isengrim was there.

'Be wary of going by yourself in these woodlands,' the wolf said. 'If you lose your way, you may not find it again.'

Silas sat down on the ground. He was too tired to stand. He felt both relieved and ashamed. Above all, he was ready to give up. Hersent was right, he thought, and Isengrim had been wrong. He could not do what the wolves needed him to do.

'I'm not ...' he said. It took a long time to get the next words out. 'Not your Wolfstongue.'

Isengrim lowered his head.

'That is for you to decide,' he said.

Isengrim led the way through the trees. Soon Silas heard the gurgling of the stream and saw the ruins of archways and pillars in the dim glade. The other animals seemed to have moved on. Isengrim prowled along the remains of a stone wall until he reached a low doorway that was still largely intact, its weathered stone lintel resting a little askew.

As Silas drew closer, he heard sounds that did not belong to the woodland. The beep of a car's horn; the hum of machines and the clatter of feet on pavement; human voices calling out, faint and distant.

'Many pathways cross here,' Isengrim said. 'You can find such places in the Forest.'

There was something odd about the doorway. It was only a remnant of stonework, nearly swallowed up by branches and leaves, but when Silas looked into the entrance a corridor reached away into darkness.

'If you want to go home, I will show you the way,' Isengrim said.

The damp bricks were low enough to brush the top of Silas's head. The smell of mildew filled his throat as he followed the wolf through several junctions, quickly forgetting the turns they took. Soon the ceiling sloped even lower, and bricks were replaced by wooden beams, and he had to move at a crouch. Finally, light glowed in the gloom, lining the edges of a rectangular panel. Silas pushed open the hatch and climbed out, coughing on dust, to a disorderly room that it took him some time to recognise as his own attic.

'Perhaps this is best, after all,' Isengrim said. 'But I am sorry.'

Still not quite sure that he was home, Silas picked his way through the old furniture and the stacks of cardboard boxes. The trapdoor lay open to the landing below. Down there was what he had almost forgotten: the ruination of the house, the filth smeared on the stairs and the slashes in the wallpaper, the shards of broken mirror scattered on the carpet. He wondered if he dared go down the steps.

Then he heard voices.

'No ... no ...'

It was Mum's voice, but different, thick and scratchy, as if she had a bad sore throat. There was a tremor in each word that Silas had never heard there before.

'No, I can't ... He's never done anything ... I don't know, I can't tell ...'

She was on the phone, he realised. She must be standing just out of sight, around the turn in the stairs.

'I don't know if he did it himself!' she was saying. 'I mean, how could he ... I don't know ...'

Mum's feet clattered away towards the bottom of the house. As her voice faded, Silas heard a quiet sobbing, broken by occasional sniffles. It was Allie. She must be in her room with the door open.

Backing away from the trapdoor, Silas heard another voice. He crossed to the small window in the gable end and stood on a crate to peer out.

Dad stood in the lane below.

'Silas!' he roared. 'SILAS!'

He took a few steps along the lane, then stopped and set off in the other direction instead, as if he were lost. His face was twisted with panic. Silas thought he was going to collapse to the ground; but instead he called out again, his voice ragged.

Now that all this was happening, Silas knew he should have foreseen it. Of course when his family came home from their trip into town and found him missing and the house vandalised, they must have imagined some strange disaster. And now he had been away for a whole night and half of another day. He had thought that somehow they would not notice he was gone, or that if they noticed they would only shrug and carry on as usual. He had not expected this consternation.

He ought to go to them at once. He had hurt them by disappearing and every moment he delayed hurt them more.

He was halfway through the trapdoor when he glanced up and saw Isengrim, still standing at the far end of the attic. Under the eyes of the wolf he could not seem to go any further: he wanted desperately to run down the stairs and tell his family that he was here and it was all right, but something would not let him. It was a horrible feeling, worse than a fox bite in the ankle, worse even than being laughed at in the school playground. In his whole life, the most important thing he had ever had to do was to go to his family right now – but he could not do it. Because if he went down now, he would never leave home again. He would always be the person who had chosen not to help the wolves find their lost children. He would live the rest of his life knowing that he had not even tried to put right the mistake that he had made.

Slowly, he climbed back into the attic and closed the trapdoor on the sound of his sister crying. He walked over to Isengrim and told the wolf what he was going to do.

Minutes later, the beams in the roof space gave way to a low, sloping mass of branches, and they were in the Forest.

'Ah,' said Tybalt. 'Wondered where you'd got to.'

The cat trotted along a branch and leaped to the next tree.

'No more delay,' Hersent said, loping past without breaking her stride. Todd came after her, and Isengrim fell in alongside the party. Silas hardly knew what had happened – what kind of choice he had just made, or what it meant – but there was no time to think about it. The animals were disappearing into the grey and green tangle of the woods.

'Hersent,' Silas said. He jogged to catch up with her.

'I'm really ... really sorry for what I did. Sorry I let the foxes in.'

Hersent kept walking, her muzzle low to the ground.

'Apologies are for humans,' she said. 'They mean nothing to wolves.'

———•———

'Picture a pine cone, pointing down, buried in the ground,' Isengrim said. 'That's the fox city. The widest part is the Upper City, where the ordinary foxes live. Then, as you go deeper, it gets narrower. That's the Lower City, where the rich, important foxes have their dens. After that you come to the Citadel, which is the buried castle from where Reynard rules the city. The Great Hall is there too, where all the foxes have to meet on special occasions.

'And lastly, below the Citadel, is the Keep. That's the prison where they're holding the pups. That's where we have to go.

'But first,' Isengrim added, 'we have to get through that gate over there.'

Silas was lying on his stomach, with the wolves to one side of him and Todd, Tybalt and Corax to the other. They were behind a ridge, spying on the entrance to the city. It did not look like much. A stone archway framed the mouth of a tunnel into the hill. A pair of black iron gates stood open, and foxes and other animals passed in and out, watched by a squad of five large foxes who were guarding the way.

'That's the city watch,' Isengrim said. 'They call them the red-collars.'

Silas saw that each of the guard-foxes wore a red band around his neck.

'Good luck getting in there,' Tybalt said. 'You're going to need it.'

Corax *toc-toc-toc*ked at the cat. 'If you're going to be so negative, why did you come?'

'I'll be all right,' Tybalt said. 'It's the rest of you that are going to get caught right away. Tell you what, bird, I'll make you a promise. If you make it out of this alive, I won't eat you for the rest of this month.'

'You wish you could eat me,' Corax said.

'If I wanted to eat you,' said Tybalt, 'you'd be ate.'

While the cat and the bird bickered, the wolves were deep in discussion with Todd.

'It's not possible,' the little fox was saying. 'Things have changed since you escaped.'

Listening, Silas gathered that there was more than one way through the city of the foxes. The direct route was the Grand Passage, a broad underground highway that spiralled like a corkscrew all the way from the surface, through the Upper City and the Lower, down to the Citadel, the deepest root of the city of Earth.

'It's the fastest way,' Isengrim said. 'We could be there in minutes.'

'But you'd never make it,' Todd said. 'They guard the Passage too well, these days. Reynard's foxes would catch you at once.'

The wolves growled, but they did not argue.

'Then we take another path,' said Hersent. 'We use the back tunnels and stay out of sight. We move fast and stay silent and let no creature get in our way.'

'We'll have to cross the Marketplace, and the Stone Gardens,' Isengrim said. 'We'll have to get through the gateway to the Lower City. And then there's Down Town and Deep Den, before we even reach the Citadel.'

'We can do all that,' Hersent said.

The wolves touched noses.

'Very well.'

'Hey,' said Corax, 'what's that?'

Three foxes had come out of the gate, hauling a battered cart on a length of rope. It was filled with dark stuff. The foxes dropped the rope and stood panting, while the guard-foxes looked it over, wrinkling their noses. Then, wearily, the three foxes began to haul it again.

'That's a night-soil cart,' said Isengrim. 'It's full of fox droppings.'

'Ugh!' Tybalt said. 'What's wrong with doing it in someone's flowerbed?'

As Silas watched, more carts and trollies passed in and out of the city. He saw a wheeled shopping bag like his granny used, and a child's toy wagon. Most of them were pulled by small teams of foxes, but other animals had been put to work too. Silas saw a goat tied between the handles of a wheelbarrow, drawing it behind him like a cart, and a glum-looking collie dog hauling an old-fashioned pram. There was even a gang of rats, ten or a dozen, scrabbling madly to drag along a wicker basket to which they had been harnessed.

'They're using human things,' Silas said.

Isengrim growled.

'Made by humans, thrown away by humans and salvaged by foxes. There are lots of things the foxes use that they can't make themselves. But humans give them everything they need. The foxes are always trying to be more like you.'

'Look there,' Hersent said.

The largest wagon yet was moving towards the gate. It was a trailer with high metal sides and an open top. It was meant to be pulled behind a car, but instead it was being dragged by a grey animal with long, drooping ears. A fox perched on his back, nipping at his shoulders.

'Baldwin the mule,' Isengrim said.

'Our way in,' said Hersent.

Hersent was whispering to Todd. The fox looked terrified.

'OK,' he said. 'I think I can do that. Maybe.'

He scurried down the ridge.

'Everyone else, follow me,' Hersent said.

She led the way along the ridge, fast and silent. She flattened herself to the ground. Peeking over, Silas saw that the mule and his trailer were going to pass close by.

'Stay hidden,' said Corax. 'I'll tell you when.'

The trailer clanked as it drew level with the place where they were hiding. The mule snorted.

'Excuse me! Hello up there!'

Silas peeked again, and saw that Todd was standing in Baldwin's path. The fox on the mule's back cursed. The mule flicked an ear.

'Out of the way! What's your problem?'

'I'm awfully sorry, sir,' said Todd. 'I don't mean to inconvenience you.'

'Well you are. Shift.'

'Of course, I'm sure you must be a very busy fox,' Todd said. His voice trembled. 'But I just need to ask for a minute of your valuable time. I, er ... I couldn't help admiring your fine cart.'

'Eh?'

'I've always wanted to drive a rubbish cart,' Todd said. 'Especially one like this, such a magnificent conveyance, pulled by such a noble beast ...'

'Think you're funny?' the driver snarled. 'Hop it or I'll run you over.'

'Coast's clear,' said Corax. 'Go now.'

They scrambled over the ridge and looked down into the trailer. It was empty except for scraps and stains, and a few small bones and feathers. The stench was disgusting. Silas thought of the big green bins at school, which filled the alley behind the dining hall with the smell of spoiled food, but this was even worse.

Hersent jumped silently into the trailer, but as Isengrim rose to follow, Baldwin the mule looked up and caught sight of him.

The wolf and the mule stared at one another. Then Baldwin flicked his ear and lowered his head. Isengrim landed beside Hersent in the trailer.

Tybalt was peering over the ridge.

'Seriously?' he said. 'This is your plan? Thanks, but no thanks. I'll find my own way in.'

This said, he was gone.

'Quick,' Corax hissed to Silas. 'Go on, jump down.'

Silas strained for words, then shook his head frantically, trying to show the raven that he could not jump as the wolves had. It was too far. Corax stared at him, but finally she understood.

'This way,' she said. She flapped to the rear of the trailer, and Silas slid down the slope after her. With fumbling fingers he opened the tailgate. Holding his breath, almost choking on the smell, he squatted beside the wolves and the raven.

'... And if I ever see you again,' the driver was saying to Todd, 'I'm going to bite off that mangy brush and shove it down your throat, understand?'

'Perfectly, sir, thank you very much,' Todd said. 'It's been most helpful to speak with you.'

The trailer rolled forwards. The driver was muttering to himself.

'Well done, fox,' Isengrim said under his breath.

A short time later the trailer stopped again, and they heard voices. The driver was speaking to the foxes guarding the gate. He sounded cross. They sounded bored. Silas held his nose. Something banged on the side of the trailer, and they trundled onwards. Shadow covered them as a roof appeared above.

'We're through,' Isengrim said. 'We're in the Earth.'

11

AS THE trailer clanked along, Silas crouched beside the wolves, breathing through his mouth and trying not to gag on the stench. He could not see over the high sides of the trailer, but he heard yelps and shouts, the rattle of wheels and the scrape of sleds on all sides. It sounded as if they were passing through a crowd. An arched ceiling of tidy red bricks was sliding past overhead. A bundle of insulated wire ran along the ceiling, strung at intervals with light bulbs of many shapes and sizes, glowing in many colours, some dim, some bright.

'Electric,' Isengrim murmured. 'That's new.'

The trailer veered to one side, and they trundled into a lower, smaller tunnel. Here the roof was not clean mortared brick but bare earth and stones, and the electric light gave way to heavy gloom. Eventually the trailer clattered to a halt, and they heard the driver grumbling as he unfastened Baldwin and led him away.

They waited until the sounds had echoed into silence. Then Silas unfastened the tailgate and they climbed down from the trailer. The driver had left it in a dead-end tunnel, in a row of empty carts stinking of rubbish.

'You took your time,' said Tybalt, who was sitting nearby. 'I was about to go home.'

Todd came around the corner and hurried to join them, his tongue lolling.

'Almost lost you,' he panted.

'My dear fellow, you don't look well,' Tybalt said. 'I think you worry too much.'

'Let's move,' Hersent said.

Silas followed the animals through a tangle of passageways. Hersent led the way, with Todd, Tybalt and Corax coming after her and Isengrim at the rear. The walls were of mud, damp and mouldy, and Silas had to stoop under the low ceilings. The only light came from wicks in old tin cans that had been left here and there on the ground, filled with what smelled like burning fat. Often it grew so dark that Silas had to reach for Isengrim's fur to make sure he did not take a wrong turning.

'These are the Shallow Tunnels,' Isengrim said. 'Just now we were in the Grand Passage, which leads straight down to the rich, beautiful parts of the city, the parts the foxes love the most. But these tunnels are part of the city too. They're the service corridors, the place where the servants do the dirty work the important foxes don't want to know about.'

Silas could hear a confused noise in the distance. It got louder as they continued along the tunnels. Then Hersent halted the party with a growl. Looking cautiously around a corner, they saw where the noise was coming from.

It was an enormous room, bigger than Silas's school sports hall, as large as the concourse of a railway station. The ceiling was held up by wooden beams and dozens of pillars that looked as if they had been cut from telegraph poles. Every inch of space was crowded with foxes: many hundreds of foxes.

'The Marketplace,' Isengrim said. 'The biggest chamber in the Upper City. We need to cross it.'

The room echoed with the barks and cackles of the foxes. It stank of fox dung and rotting food. All over the place foxes were eating, sleeping, talking and fighting. A gang of fox cubs played, chasing one another in and out of the shell of a big old-fashioned television. Many foxes had built shelters from cardboard boxes or old clothes or other bits of human refuse. Some were lying in these shabby hideouts, looking sick, half-starved or hopeless; some were arguing viciously, snarling and snapping over a scrap of food, a spot to lie down in or nothing at all. Silas had not been sure what to expect of the foxes' city, but he certainly had not imagined it would be like this.

'We're getting too crowded,' Todd said. 'More and more foxes have nowhere to make their dens. So they're living in the Marketplace. It's not good.'

Elsewhere in the huge chamber, foxes were trading. Silas saw one fox swap a dead sparrow for another fox's punnet of mouldy strawberries, and two more foxes were haggling over the exchange of half a rat for a bicycle wheel. He saw foxes using all manner of human devices. One fox held a can opener to a tin of beans while another fox turned the handle; one fox held a book open while another tore the pages out and crumpled them up for bedding; two foxes wove their heads around one another as they wrapped a pink butcher's bone in brown paper and tied it up with a length of string. It seemed there was nothing that human hands could do that could not be done just as well by the jaws of foxes working skilfully together.

Here and there, large foxes in red collars were patrolling the Marketplace. They held their heads high, scanning the chamber for anything amiss. One of them broke up a fight between two young foxes, knocking both down. Another helped himself to a piece of bacon fat that a skinny old fox was offering to a pup. The Marketplace foxes kept their heads down as the red-collars passed.

'You know,' Tybalt said, 'I'm really looking forward to seeing how you get through here without a hundred foxes raising the alarm. Because if they do that, it's bye-bye wolf pups.'

'He's right,' Corax said. 'No way through.'

The wolves studied the throng of foxes. It seemed to Silas that they were looking in particular at one very fat fox who was standing nearby, facing out across the Marketplace with his back to the tunnel entrance. He was in charge of a tall, wobbly heap of wooden cages: hundreds of them, precariously piled, each no larger than a shoebox.

Isengrim looked at Hersent.

'Do it,' she said.

Leaving the rest of the party in the tunnel, Isengrim began to creep around the edge of the Marketplace. He kept low and wove his way towards the heap of wooden cages. Foxes were queuing up to barter with the fat fox, Silas saw. There was fluttering movement inside the cages.

'Do those cages have *chickens* inside?'

'The foxes farm them,' Corax said. 'Those birds are hatched down here. They spend their lives caged, never getting out, never getting sunlight or fresh air, never flapping their wings or walking a step. Then, one day, they're dinner.'

Isengrim was behind the teetering heap of cages. He paused. Then he jumped, knocking the cages on top of the fat fox and his customers.

Within moments everything was in chaos. Isengrim was breaking open the cages, letting out a boiling mass of wings, beaks, claws and feathers. Hundreds of chickens exploded into the room, their eyes rolling with panic.

Neither foxes nor chickens knew what was going on. Fox jaws closed on bird necks. Beaks jabbed and claws raked. The roof rang with screeching and the air filled with feathers. It was a battle. Red-collared foxes hurried over to see what was going on, but they were engulfed by the bloody scrum.

Silas and his companions dashed through the confusion and into a tunnel mouth at the far side of the Marketplace.

———◆———

The wolves led the way through another snarl of tunnels. Within minutes Silas lost his bearings again.

'This is the Upper Warren,' Todd said. 'Not a nice part of town.'

A rotten stench rose from the chewed chicken bones, scraps of fur and feather, old rags and fox droppings that were strewn across the floor. Every few feet, smaller holes opened in the sides of the passageway. Silas could hear scrabbling nearby, and when he peered into one of the holes he was met with reflecting eyes in the darkness.

'Just keep moving,' Todd hissed. 'Believe me, they don't care.'

As the party turned a corner, they stumbled on an elderly fox who lay sprawled across the tunnel floor. He blinked at them, unconcerned, as they went by.

Further twists and turns brought them into a larger chamber. Spaced around it were six large pieces of pale stone, irregular in shape, each one taller than Silas. They served no purpose that he could make out, but they had obviously been positioned with care. Smooth pebbles lay in decorative rings around their bases. Flecks of mica sparkled in the rock, picked out by lamps that glowed in globes of coloured glass on the ceiling.

'The Stone Gardens,' Isengrim said. 'We can move fast, but we must be stealthy.'

The Stone Gardens, Silas now discovered, were a series of linked chambers and corridors in which all manner of rocks had been gathered and displayed. Left to himself, he would soon have been going around in circles, but the wolves led the way without hesitation through a miniature mineral wonderland. The foxes had arranged trunks and arches of sandstone, cool limestone boulders and pillars of dark granite alongside hexagonal basalt columns, mushroom-like blobs of bubbled stone and smooth rock cylinders that seemed to have melted like candles; and among these larger forms, Silas saw formations of deep blue azurite and turquoise malachite as intricate as origami, frail clusters of scolecite needles like dandelion clocks, beds of geodes split like melons to show interiors of purple amethyst and emerald green; he saw gleaming swords of crystal quartz, raw opals with rainbows caught in their substance, chunks of pink rhodochrosite with the delicate translucency of Turkish delight, obsidian lumps whose black depths seemed to glow with veins of red, and milk-white calcite grown into structures like elaborate coral.

'Pretty, isn't it?' Todd said. 'I eat my lunch here sometimes.'

Beyond the Stone Gardens they came to another zone of tunnels, but these were not so cramped and dark, nor so smelly, as the Upper Warren. Here the tunnel floors were hard earth, smoothly packed and swept clean, and the openings of the foxholes were neat and regular: most had scraps of fabric pinned up to cover their entrances.

Todd was still walking beside Silas.

'I live round here,' he said. 'Middle Burrows isn't fancy, but it's a decent neighbourhood.'

He thought.

'I mean, I used to live here. Suppose I won't be coming back.'

The wolves were padding forward cautiously, with the rest of the party close behind. They paused at the corners and intersections, alert for signs of life, but they encountered no-one.

'Where are the foxes?' Hersent said. 'It shouldn't be this empty.'

The wolves looked at Todd, but the little fox shook his head.

Just then, a voice called out behind them.

'Halt!' it said. 'Stop right there!'

They turned to see that two red-collars had come around the corner. They were members of the city watch, but they did not look as tough as the red-collared foxes that had been guarding the entrance to the city, or those who had been patrolling the Marketplace. These two were an odd-looking pair. One was small and plump, while the other was long and thin, with a startled look to his pointed face.

'Halt!' said the thin fox.

'I already said halt,' the plump one said.

'Sorry. OK then. Er. Halt!'

The plump fox rolled his eyes.

'Only foxes are allowed this deep in the city,' said the thin fox. 'No outside animals. And ...' He looked at the group carefully. 'Some of you aren't foxes, are you?'

The plump fox sighed. '*Obviously* they're not foxes,' he said.

'Right,' the thin fox said. 'Obviously. I knew that.'

Isengrim and Hersent were circling towards the two guard-foxes. The plump fox glanced around, but the thin fox kept talking.

'And since you're not foxes, I must ask you to come with us, so we can ... er ...'

The thin fox began to look worried. He swallowed as Isengrim came closer. Hersent was behind the foxes by now, cutting off their retreat.

'So we can take you to the ... er ... the station, for ... um ... processing.'

The watch-foxes looked at one another nervously. The wolves were almost on top of them now, teeth bared, eyes hard. Silas held his breath, wishing the two foxes had not spotted the party, or had been wise enough to carry on their patrol without calling out a challenge. Their faces, thin and plump, were puzzled, as if they were starting to suspect that they had wandered into a situation that might not be so easy to get out of.

Then Todd spoke.

'Actually, officers, we are all foxes here.'

The red-collared foxes looked at him in surprise. So did the wolves.

'Oh, yes,' said Todd. 'As you can see, my two friends here, who are so keen to introduce themselves, are unusually large, grey foxes. They're visiting from a far-off part of the Forest. They've never seen real city foxes.

That's why they're so thrilled to meet you.'

Relief dawned on the foxes' faces.

'Aah,' said the thin one.

'Right,' the plump one said. But he looked with confusion at the rest of the party.

'And this,' said Todd, glancing at Silas, 'is a rare kind of fox that walks on his hind legs. A rare, upright-walking, hairless, clothes-wearing monkey-fox.'

'From really ... really far away,' Silas said.

'Wow!' said the thin fox. 'And this here must be a flying fox?'

'An extremely rare miniature black-feathered flying fox,' Todd said.

Corax bowed.

'Pleased to meet you, fellow foxes.'

'Visiting from very far away?' asked the plump fox.

'Why, yes!'

The red-collared foxes nodded slowly.

'Well,' said the plump one. 'I suppose that all makes sense ...'

'Hey, don't forget about me,' Tybalt said. 'I'm, like, a cat-fox.'

'Yes. Right. OK,' said the plump fox. 'Well, everything seems to be in order here. Carry on about your business, brothers and sisters, and enjoy your visit to the city of Earth.'

'I'll make sure they do, officer,' Todd said.

They had turned to go when another shout came from the guard-foxes.

'Hey! Hey, you, stop!'

The party froze, and dread clutched at Silas's stomach.

'I almost forgot,' said the plump fox, bustling towards them again. 'You shouldn't be here.'

Silas heard the snarl start up in Isengrim's throat, but the plump fox carried on.

'It's by order of Brother Reynard,' he said. 'Every fox in the City of Earth is instructed to report immediately for a Full Assembly in the Great Hall. You have to go there without delay.'

The thin fox sniggered and nudged his comrade.

'Can't believe you forgot that,' he said.

The plump fox frowned at the thin one.

'It's lucky you ran into us,' he said. 'We're just making a last round of the Burrows to call out stragglers. You need to get down to the Grand Passage and join the queue for the gate.'

Todd was nodding energetically.

'Yes, officer,' he said. 'Lucky we ran into you. Can't think how we missed that news. We'll get down there at once.'

'And keep your eyes peeled for any animals who aren't foxes,' said the thin fox. 'You can't be too careful.'

'Thanks so much, officer,' Todd said.

With that, the foxes of the city watch continued in one direction, and the wolves' party continued in the other.

———◆———

'That explains where the foxes went,' Hersent said.

The whole party – Hersent and Isengrim, Silas, Tybalt, Corax and Todd – hid around the bend of a tunnel that opened into the Grand Passage. When Silas had sneaked a glance out, he had seen a wide, arched, brick-lined corridor lit by electric bulbs. The corridor was filled, all the way until it curved out of sight, with a huge crowd of foxes, jostling and grumbling as they queued to pass through a set of gates. The gates, a pair of heavy oak doors inside a pointed arch, looked as if they might have once belonged to a church or a town hall. When closed they would block the Passage, but just now they stood open, and squads of red-collars kept watchful eyes on the crowd as it passed through.

'That's the Lower City Gate,' Isengrim said.

'I've never seen it this busy,' Todd said. 'How are we going to get through?'

'Let me get this straight,' said Tybalt. 'It just so happens that every fox in the city is being summoned to a big town meeting, right now? Tell me, little buddy, do the foxes have these get-togethers often?'

'Not often,' said Todd. 'I've only ever been to one. That was when we all agreed Reynard should be leader of the city.'

Tybalt smiled.

'And now they're having another, today of all days.'

'Good luck, maybe,' Corax said. 'At least we know they're busy.'

'I don't like it,' Hersent said. 'But it makes no difference.'

Isengrim growled his agreement. 'We go on.'

'How?' asked Todd.

'Follow me.'

Hersent turned back along the tunnel, then led them through a side entrance that Silas had not noticed. They crossed a wooden bridge and came to a passage that was half-filled with water: an underground canal. A walkway ran down one side.

'This is the way through.'

Hersent touched her nose to the surface of the water, then turned to Todd.

'What do you know about these canals?'

'I know they run all the way through the city,' he said. 'The water comes from somewhere below and gets drawn up to the surface.'

Hersent growled.

'They say the only way from the Upper City to the Lower is through the Gate,' she said. 'But it's not that simple. When the foxes built this place, they found they had to make all sorts of extra channels and passages. They needed rubbish chutes and chimneys to get rid of the smoke from their lamps. And they needed to carry water from the sources deep down underground to the upper levels, so they built a system of canals, pipes and waterwheels. Look there.'

At the end of the canal tunnel a wooden construction hung above the water. It was like a giant hamster wheel, suspended from a stout axle in the wall, with space inside for a large animal.

'I used to walk in this wheel,' Hersent said.

A canvas belt ran around the bottom of the wheel and disappeared into a shaft above. Buckets were fixed to the outside of the belt.

Hersent climbed into the wheel and began to walk. As the wheel turned and the belt moved, Silas saw how the machine worked. The buckets came down the shaft and around the bottom of the wheel, dipping into the water. Then full buckets rose on the other side and began to move up the shaft. The turning of the wheel carried water upward through the city.

'When the system is running, you need an animal in every wheel,' Hersent said. 'This canal is fed by the wheel below. Then this wheel lifts the water to the next canal. And so on, until you get to the top.'

Hersent was walking faster now. The full buckets swayed as they climbed into the shaft.

'This section of canal connects the Lower and the Upper City.'

Hersent began to run.

'There's a closed pipe that carries the water between the two parts of the city,' she said, raising her voice now to be heard over the creaking of the wheel. 'You couldn't get through it when it's full of water.'

The buckets rose, swaying and splashing. The level of the water had fallen.

'But if I drain this canal, we can go along the channel and through the pipe. We'll come out in the Lower City.'

The wheel whirred.

'I can see the bottom,' Todd said. By now the water was only ankle-deep. Rubble littered the canal bed, mixed with an assortment of junk: a broken broom handle, a wire shopping basket, a scattering of jam jars, a greenish length of copper tube.

'Start walking,' Hersent called.

Silas climbed down behind Isengrim and the others. The buckets no longer touched the water. The wheel squeaked as Hersent sped up. There was a crack, and the wheel shifted a little on its axle.

Isengrim looked up at his mate.

'Hersent?' he said. 'The canal's drained. You can stop.'

'Start walking,' she barked.

The wheel cracked again. Its spokes were a blur and its noise had become a harsh groan. They set off along the channel, with the wheel roaring behind them and the wolf pounding at full pelt inside it.

When the final, splintering crack came, they turned in time to see the wheel break loose from its axle and career into the canal bed. When it landed, it smashed, releasing a wolf who did not stop running but galloped past them, splashing through shallow water, tearing towards her pups, running like a wolf who meant never to stop until she had found them.

———•———

Down here, the foxes' city was no longer a place of dark, smelly tunnels. Hersent led the way along wide, regular corridors like underground streets. They walked on pavement, between brick walls on which oil lamps glowed. Silas knew he was deep underground, but he had the strange feeling that he could almost be back on the surface. The ceiling of pale blue tiles was so high that he did not have to stoop. He paused to look at a fox-sized front door, painted pea green. It had a brass knocker, a letterbox and a doorknob polished so well that he could see a distorted reflection of his face.

'The Down Town foxes make their dens like human dwellings,' Isengrim said.

'Yeah, it's the one fashion they never get tired of,' Todd said. 'I've never really seen the point, myself, but what would I know?'

Street signs were attached to the walls at corners and junctions. The signs were all different, some big and some small, some metal, some wooden and some plastic. Silas saw streets called Ngumba Road, Polding Avenue, Calle San Javier and Ulitsa Borovaya. The foxes must have taken them from lots of different human towns.

Tybalt and Corax scouted ahead of the others. Several times they heard the chatter of foxes passing, and hung back until the way was clear. They hid in an alley while two foxes went by, pulling a small cart loaded with brushes and bins.

'We'll finish Chalcedony Crescent,' one of them was saying to the other as they passed. 'Then we'd best get down to the Hall.'

A minute later Tybalt hustled the party behind a corner. They held their breaths as a squad of eight foxes marched past. They were heavily built, rust-red animals. Each wore a white collar.

'Elite guard,' Todd whispered. 'They make me nervous.'

'What doesn't?' Tybalt said.

Every now and then, a spiral staircase or a ramp took them deeper into the city. At last the underground streets opened into a chamber. It was much smaller than the Upper City Marketplace, but it was far grander. The floor was paved with a chessboard of black and white marble. Slender pillars supported a high ceiling and long balconies ran along the sides of the room.

'This is the Low Plaza,' Todd said. 'Very posh. Likes of me shouldn't be here. It's where the Deep Den types come to show off to one another.'

Hersent pointed to an archway on the far side.

'The Citadel Gate is just beyond,' she said. 'That's the final gate in the Grand Passage. It's where all the foxes will be passing through to the Great Hall.'

'Again, I have to ask,' Tybalt said. 'Do we really feel it's a coincidence that all this is happening today?'

'*Kraa*,' said Corax. 'Sure it's fine.'

'If the foxes are distracted, we have to make the most of it,' Isengrim said. 'We take our chance.'

'All the same to me,' said Tybalt. 'Tell you what, though, I'm going to check out this gate. You lot can stay here.'

Before anyone could reply, the cat darted across the chamber and vanished through the archway.

As they waited, Silas admired the chandeliers that hung on silver chains from the vaulted ceiling of the

Plaza: frozen bursts of crystal that shed soft light across the chamber. Statues stood here and there on the marble pavement. They were statues of human beings, but their heads had been removed and replaced with the heads of foxes, fashioned from various materials: some had been chiselled from lumps of stone or carved from wood, and one was the blade of a large steel shovel which had been beaten into shape.

'The cat's been too long,' Hersent muttered.

'Give him time,' Isengrim said. 'It's why he's here.'

Then they heard a voice.

'I say! You! The scruffy fox!'

Todd looked frantically around. Silas could not tell where the voice was coming from either; then he saw a fox on the balcony above them.

'Yes, you, the shabby little one,' the fox said. 'What are you doing?'

The fox peered over the bannister at the companions. He was a very well-turned-out fox, with gleaming fur, a bow of lavender silk around his neck and a gold ring in his ear.

'Good gracious me,' he said. 'Those are wolves, aren't they? I know who you are. You're here because of those wolf pups.'

'Um,' said Todd. 'Wolf pups? What wolf pups?'

'Please, don't make me laugh,' said the fox. 'They're all anyone's talking about. Everyone thinks the wolf pups are the reason Brother Reynard has called this Assembly. And you: you're obviously a traitor fox, helping our enemies, trying to steal them away. I shall summon the guard at once.'

He strolled towards a doorway.

'Wait!' called Todd. 'You mustn't!'

The fox on the balcony laughed.

'What's to stop me? You're not in the Upper City now. This is Deep Den. When I call out, this place will be full of white-collars in no time. I'll probably get a reward.'

Corax flapped up towards the balcony, but the fox snapped at her and she circled away again. The wolves were ranging back and forth, seeking a way up, but the well-groomed fox was out of reach. Silas could see no way of stopping him from raising the alarm.

Laughing, the fox stepped through the doorway.

As he did so, Tybalt dropped on him from above. The cat bit the fox once in the back of the neck. The fox fell without a sound.

'Sheesh,' Tybalt said, stepping away. 'I can't leave you bozos alone for a minute, can I?'

He leaped from the balcony to the head of a statue, then down to the floor.

'So anyway,' he said. 'I had a peek. The Citadel Gate. The gate's open, but you've got about fifty of those tough guys in the white collars, standing in lines on either side of it in a stiff kind of way. And then you've got every last fox in the city coming down the Passage and going through. Basically, there's no way you're getting in there without being seen by a squillion foxes.'

He stretched, arching his back.

'Sorry, wolves. End of the line.'

Isengrim shook his head.

'I know another way.'

12

ISENGRIM LED them onwards through the Lower City. Now they went along wide underground streets where the houses of important foxes were built of white stone. Now golden light glowed from brass lamp-posts, and bunches of fragrant herbs stood in glazed pots on every corner. Now they came to a smaller street, and now to a low door.

'A group of foxes lives in here,' Isengrim said. 'They're the humblest foxes in Deep Den, but all the other foxes admire them. Or they say they do.'

He glanced at Silas.

'If they were humans, they would be called monks. They never leave their house. They think they can't leave, because their duty is too important.'

'What's their duty?'

'They are the Keepers of the Words.'

Isengrim led them into a long bare stone room, lit by a few oil lamps. Two rows of foxes lined the sides of the room. They sat with their heads bowed and eyes closed, facing the walls. The room was filled with the whispering echoes of their voices.

Silas could not tell whether the foxes noticed as the party tiptoed down the room behind their backs. If they noticed, none gave any sign. They muttered on and on, so absorbed in what they were saying that it seemed nothing could break their concentration. Silas caught snatches of their words.

'... Reached out and plucked the grapes ...'

'... So they lifted the sharp stake and hardened it in the fire ...'

'... Never, said the fox, by my body and soul, have I wronged you in any way ...'

'... Took the bone and fashioned it into a pipe ...'

Isengrim was nosing at an iron ring in the floor. He took it between his teeth and pulled, opening a trapdoor. Next he picked up one of the oil lamps. Silas saw that these had been made for animals to carry: they were fashioned from old jam jars and syrup tins, and each had a long wooden grip covered in tooth marks.

One by one the party climbed down. Silas went last and closed the trap behind him.

Isengrim set down his lamp. The light showed a tunnel ahead.

'Most foxes think the Citadel is impregnable,' Isengrim said. 'They think you can't get in or out unless Reynard lets you. But I built the place, and I know its secrets. Reynard could not bear the idea of a fortress with only one door. He could think of too many reasons he might want to get in or out without passing through the public gate. So he added a secret passage.'

He picked up the oil lamp in his teeth. The tunnel wound back and forth and up and down and finally brought them to another trapdoor. Climbing up after the others, Silas found they were in a tiny room filled with buckets and mops.

The companions crept from the store cupboard into a corridor that was perhaps the strangest sight Silas had seen in the city of the foxes. The floor was covered with grey carpet. The walls were painted pale beige. Electric lamps shed an even light. It was exactly like a corridor you might see in a particularly boring human building. It reminded Silas of times when he had visited his mum or his dad at the offices where they worked, except that these corridors were shrunken to half the size. The ceiling brushed his head.

Here and there, bright green plants stood in pots, but when he looked closer Silas saw that they were made of plastic. Framed watercolour paintings hung on the walls, but whoever had painted them was not a very good artist, Silas thought, and their choice of subject was odd. Each painting showed foxes dressed up in small versions of human clothes, doing human things like driving cars, having picnics, playing golf, riding horses, planting a flag on the summit of a mountain. Silas did not think the foxes really did any of these things, and they certainly did not wear clothes.

The party ducked back into the storeroom as four white-collared foxes tramped past.

'Stay close,' Isengrim said. 'I know the way.'

The Citadel was bustling. Voices argued just out of sight, tails disappeared around corners, doors slammed: the foxes who worked in the Citadel sounded flustered and excited, as though something out of the ordinary was going on. Isengrim led the way through the corridors, never hesitating, sometimes sprinting across an open stretch, sometimes ducking into a hiding place. Whenever Silas thought they were about to be spotted, Isengrim turned another way and their path was clear.

Finally they came to a stairwell, lit by a bare bulb. The steps led down to a small landing and a single door.

'This is it,' Isengrim said. 'The Keep.'

The door was a slab of iron, set in a stone wall. Its only feature was a keyhole.

'I didn't know what to expect here,' Isengrim went on.

'But I know there's no other way through. No tricks or secret passages.'

'We find the key, then,' said Hersent.

'Agreed,' Isengrim said. 'It must be somewhere in the Citadel.'

They looked at Todd, but the fox shook his head.

'I've no idea,' he said.

'We go back up,' Hersent said. 'We catch a fox who does know, and make it tell us. We catch as many as we need to.'

'I like it,' said Tybalt. 'Let's go.'

Corax flapped uneasily, but gave a *kraa* of agreement.

The wolves turned back up the stairwell, but Silas called after them.

'Wait!'

He was touching the door. It drifted on its hinges.

'You don't need a key,' he said. 'It's open.'

A spiral staircase wound downwards. The chill of the stone shaft engulfed them like deep water. Silas wondered how far under the ground they had come.

At the bottom they found a bare room with a floor of packed earth. An iron shackle was fixed to the wall, and a single heavy chain ran from the shackle through rings on the collars of the three wolf pups.

They lay in a heap of grubby fur, looking smaller than before. They raised their heads blearily, but a moment later they were hauling at the chain, yipping and squealing, trying to get to their parents.

As Hersent started across the room towards them, a fox came from a side door. It was Saffron. When she saw the wolves, she froze, and Silas thought she was going to run. But then she bared her teeth in a sneer.

'If it isn't Hersent, the one-eyed she-wolf!' she said. 'Come to visit me and my babies.'

She strolled over to the pups. They shrank from her and fell silent.

'We've been having a lovely time, haven't we? I've been taking such good care of them.'

Hersent stood stock-still as Saffron circled the pups. The

fox snapped at one of them and tugged hard at a knot in the small wolf's fur.

'They were ill-mannered little monsters when they got here, but it's amazing what some tough love will do. Here, watch this.'

She rapped another one of the pups on the nose.

'You. Sit up and beg.'

The small wolf looked bewildered. Saffron rapped her nose again.

'Beg!'

Trembling, the small wolf tried to stand on her hind legs. But she could not find her balance, and Saffron, losing patience, knocked her to the ground.

'Ugh. Well, we've barely started. There's plenty of time.'

She gave Hersent a sly look.

'I'm so glad you're here. We can talk about these things, one mum to another. Do you know what I find tricky? Names. I can't decide what to call them. But I think I've narrowed it down. I'm going to call them Ugly, Weak and Stupid. I just haven't decided yet which is which.'

She prodded the nearest pup.

'Which will you be?'

Then Saffron straightened up. Hersent was padding closer.

'What have we here?' Saffron said. 'The angry snarl? The hackles raised?'

Saffron narrowed her green eyes.

'Do you think I'm scared of an old, blind wolf?'

Hersent gathered her body into a crouch, but it was obvious now that she was exhausted. Her every movement was clumsy and slow, and even Silas could see what she was going to do before she did it. She blundered into the middle of the room, almost losing her balance, and looked around in confusion. The fox had skipped easily out of her reach.

Saffron circled Hersent, and the wolf swung her head laboriously as she tried to keep the fox in sight. Then Saffron lunged at Hersent's blind side, quick as the stab of a knife. She darted away with blood trailing from her mouth. Hersent had not tried to fight back.

Saffron laughed.

'I know how to kill a wolf. I've been killing them for ever.'

She showed her teeth.

'I'm Saffron the fox.'

Twice more she bobbed past Hersent's weary jaws to draw blood from her flanks. Then she ducked with ease under a heavy paw and slashed the wolf's nose. At that, Hersent seemed to lose all hope. She only stood there with blood dripping from her face to the earth.

'In the old days, when wolves were worn out and no more use, I was the one who finished them off,' Saffron said. 'That was good. You remind me of them: an old, blind wolf who can't even take care of her mangy whelps.'

Hersent's head swung slowly from side to side. The fox danced around her, laughing.

'Watch closely, kids,' Saffron said to the pups. 'This is how you do it. First you bleed them, tire them out. And when you've had your fun, you finish. Like so.'

The fox sauntered forward, licking her chops. Silas, appalled, moved to interrupt, but Isengrim gave a soft warning growl.

And then Hersent moved more quickly than Silas could follow. It was impossible to see how, but all at once the wolf's jaws were clamped in the fox's throat.

Saffron's tongue quivered. Her eyes bulged. Her back legs pedalled as she was lifted clear of the floor. She tried to speak, but no sound came. Froth ran from her mouth. The green eyes rolled, and for an instant they found Silas. If they held a message, he could not tell what it was.

Hersent wrenched her jaws upwards and a curved blade of blood cut the air. An object hit the ceiling, bounced off the floor and rolled into a corner.

Hersent tossed the fox's body after it.

She went to her pups. They jumped up at her, tugging at their chains and licking the blood from her jaws. Isengrim joined her, and the others watched as the family of wolves nuzzled and licked one another, squeaking with joy.

'Aw,' said Tybalt.

The wolves were tugging at the chain and biting at the pups' thick leather collars. Their teeth scraped on the metal but they could not work out how to get the pups free.

Todd's tail twitched.

'We should leave now,' he said. 'I really think we should leave.'

'A wise suggestion,' said a voice behind them. 'But not possible.'

Reynard the fox stood in the doorway, while dozens of white-collared foxes trooped past him into the room. Three of them darted straight to the iron shackle in the wall and, cooperating skilfully, used their jaws to unfasten the chain. A second later they had jerked the pups away from their parents and dragged them out of reach.

'I'm so pleased you made it,' Reynard said. 'Now, let's get down to business, shall we?'

13

THE CAPTIVES stood surrounded by foxes.

'Think before you act,' Reynard said. 'We don't want anyone hurt.'

The wolf pups were held tight by the necks, sharp teeth digging into their fur.

'Honestly, thanks for dealing with Saffron,' Reynard said. 'She was a dangerous fool, and she was becoming a problem. But now she's a hero who was killed by savages. Her loss will bring the city together. I've already written a speech.'

He circled the captives, looking at each in turn. From Hersent to Isengrim, to Silas, Tybalt and Corax. Then to Todd, who seemed to shrink under Reynard's eye.

'Ah, yes, Todd,' he said. 'You weren't part of my plan to begin with, but your contribution has not gone unnoticed. When you started sneaking around, we spotted you at once, of course, but I decided not to arrest you right away. I let you leave the city, because I had an idea you might help bring me these wolves. And what do you know?'

Todd stared at Reynard, dumbfounded.

'For you, the ending is rather harsh, I'm afraid,' Reynard said. 'You see, we can't allow foxes to turn against the city. We have to make an example of you. It's going to be the full works in the Great Hall. Then we'll put what's left of you on display, to remind every fox of the virtue of loyalty.'

Two of the white-collars grabbed Todd by the ears. He began to babble and plead, but fell quiet when one of his captors boxed him in the nose.

'And then we have Corax the raven,' Reynard said. 'I must admit, I had my doubts. I wasn't sure you'd do it. But here we are, just as planned. Come on, now, don't be shy.'

Corax hopped over to stand beside Reynard, looking embarrassed.

'Corax?' said Isengrim.

'He'd already guessed what you were going to do,' the raven said. 'He knew you'd come for the pups. My job was just to make sure you did it right. See you made it all the way here.'

'Naughty, naughty!' said Tybalt, smiling.

'You always said ravens and wolves look out for one another,' Hersent snarled. 'You liar.'

'Trying to help you,' Corax said. 'Doing what's best for everyone.'

'You betrayed us!'

'Be realistic,' Corax said. 'You and your pups are the last of your kind in the Forest. There's no future for your species out there. But if you stay here and accept what the foxes are offering – then you have a future. Your pups will have pups, and those pups will have pups. They may not exactly be wolves any longer, but at least they'll be something. And if they have to serve the foxes, that won't be so bad, will it? It'll make life easier for them in the end.'

'We trusted you,' Hersent said.

Corax fluffed her feathers.

'Doing what's best. Sorry if you can't see it.'

'Sound insights there,' Reynard said. 'But enough chatter. Go ahead, officer.'

Corax squawked as one of the foxes trapped her under his paw.

'Don't worry,' Reynard said. 'You're not in the same fix as poor old Todd. False foxes must suffer, but the treachery of ravens is no concern of mine. So for you the end can be quick.'

'I helped you!'

'And now your helpfulness is at an end,' Reynard said. 'When you're ready, officer.'

But before the white-collared fox could bite down on the bird, claws raked his face. Tybalt hissed, and Corax flapped to the ceiling, shedding feathers.

'He told me the foxes would hunt down every last raven!' she squawked. 'I didn't have a choice!'

She disappeared up the staircase. Tybalt smiled at the fox he had clawed.

'That's odd, isn't it?' he said. 'I couldn't let you eat that bird. I suppose it must be because I'm planning to eat her myself, one of these days.'

The white-collared fox licked at his wounded muzzle. More foxes closed in around Tybalt. The cat stood stiff-legged, the fur bristling along his back to the tip of his tail.

'Not letting it go, eh?'

Tybalt flattened his ears, the whole one and the torn, against his head.

'Oh, very well, then.'

The cat and the foxes became a whirl of violence. Yowls and shrieks filled the room as Tybalt twisted, squirmed, dodged, hissed and spat. His claws slashed blood from a fox's ear and his teeth met in a fox's throat. For a short time it seemed that he was too fast and fierce for them to touch him. But more foxes piled in, and the cat was lost under the rust-red bodies.

'Thank you so much, officers,' Reynard said. 'That's the distractions dealt with. Now, then. If you could bring me my wolf pups.'

The foxes unfastened the pups' collars from the chain, then dragged them over to Reynard.

'I'm offering you wolves a choice.'

The only ones left in the middle of the room now were the wolves and Silas. The pups' captors gripped them by the necks. Silas did not dare move.

'It's up to you. Either these puppies die right now, or you and your offspring stay here to serve the foxes.'

Reynard's voice was friendly and calm. The kind of voice you want to trust.

'And you belong to me for ever.'

'No!' Silas shouted. He had been struggling to speak ever since Reynard had come into the room, and he was startled to hear himself manage it. 'That's not ... not a choice!'

'Silas, I'm disappointed,' Reynard said. 'Haven't you learned that when you open your mouth you only make things worse for yourself?'

Silas felt the familiar shameful heat flush through his face. Reynard watched, then turned to the wolves.

'Isengrim. Hersent. It's time to decide. Do they live or die?'

The foxes jerked the pups' heads up, showing their puzzled faces to their parents.

'I don't like this fighting any more than you do,' Reynard said. 'Just agree that the foxes are your masters, and we can all be friends again.'

There was a silence. Then Isengrim drew himself up and looked to Silas. Hersent followed his gaze. Slowly, Silas realised what they wanted. He was meant to say something. This was his chance to put right everything he had done wrong. Reynard had trapped the wolves and they could see no way out, and so it was up to Silas to be the good talker Isengrim believed he was. He must speak for the wolves, and find the words that would save them. He closed his eyes and took a deep breath – but it was no good. He did not know what to say. He made an apologetic sound, small, wordless and meaningless.

The wolves hung their heads.

'Time to decide,' said Reynard, and now there was an edge in his voice. 'I will not ask again.'

Isengrim's muzzle touched the floor.

'You are our master,' he said.

'Good,' Reynard said. 'Hersent?'

'We are your slaves,' she said.

'Very good!'

Reynard looked around brightly.

'Officers, you can put those pups down. And do be gentle. They're valuable, you know.'

The foxes dropped the pups and took hold of their chains.

'This calls for a celebration. Come, my friends. Come along, wolves.'

Isengrim and Hersent slunk to his heel.

A procession climbed the staircase out of the Keep. Reynard led the way, flanked by his guards and followed by the obedient wolves. Then came the wolf pups, their captors dragging them by the scruffs of their necks. Then Todd, tugged by the ear, and Silas, driven by nips from the guard-foxes around his legs.

Todd whimpered. 'Oh no,' he said, as they came up into the corridors of the Citadel. 'No no.'

'Quiet, traitor,' said one of the guards.

They reached a set of double doors. At the sight of what lay beyond, Todd gave a cry and tore his ear free. He dived between two of the foxes, but he had no real hope of escape. There was nowhere for him to go. They caught him and dragged him through the doors.

The foxes drove Silas after him.

'Welcome to the Great Hall,' said Reynard.

Silas and the other prisoners found themselves in the middle of an amphitheatre: a large room shaped like a deep bowl, with a flat, circular arena at the bottom. Four huge stone pillars supported the roof, and the sides of the room sloped steeply upwards on all sides, ringed with rows upon rows of seating.

Almost every seat was occupied. Silas and the others had entered directly into the arena, but there were other doors high above, at the top of the room's sloping sides: foxes were still coming through those doors and crowding into the seats beside their fellows. The room was loud with the impatient chatter of foxes. Rank fox smell filled the air, mingling with a colder, deeper scent of earth and stone from the sand under Silas's feet. Thousands of foxes stared down at the arena where the prisoners stood.

'Well met, my sisters,' Reynard said. 'My brothers, well met.'

At these words, the room fell silent. Reynard had not spoken loudly, but it seemed his voice had rung out from everywhere at once. Every last fox leaned forward to listen.

'The Great Hall of the City of Earth,' Reynard said. 'This is the place where we foxes gather for the occasions that matter the most to us. The occasions that shape our lives together and our future as a species.'

It must be the shape of the room, Silas thought. Reynard sounded calm and composed, even quiet, as if he were just having an ordinary conversation, but the amphitheatre was sounding out his words like a gigantic bell.

'Sisters and brothers, it is for just such an occasion that we are gathered here today.'

A ripple of talk went around the amphitheatre. Reynard let it pass, and went on:

'Sisters and brothers, some of you may recognise these animals. These wolves. These fearsome beasts that we foxes have tried so hard to help. I have much to tell you, my sisters and brothers, of how these wolves and their accomplices plotted against our way of life, and of how, through the courage and quick thinking of our security services, their plan was foiled – though not, alas, before it cost the lives of brave foxes.'

He shook his head, and for a few moments he seemed too upset to continue.

'All of this I shall make clear in good time,' he said. 'But first there is a more pressing matter. I see the question in your faces, sisters and brothers, and now I shall answer it.'

He turned to the guards.

'Take the wolves to one side, and the traitor too,' he said. 'Bring forth the human child.'

They shoved Silas to the centre of the arena. He tripped and fell, then scrambled to his feet, his palms stinging. Countless eyes stared down at him from every part of the Hall. He could not bear to meet those eyes, but there was no way to escape them. His cheeks burned and darkness crept in at the edges of his vision.

'You didn't think it was just about bringing back some runaway wolves, did you?' Reynard said.

He had dropped his voice now, so that his words no longer resonated around the Hall. He was speaking so that only Silas could hear.

'That was a minor issue,' he said. 'It had to be done, but my real plan goes further. You see, Silas, it's really about you.'

14

'ONCE, WHEN the Forest was young,' said Reynard, 'there was a fox.'

His voice was strong and clear. It was not only the shape of the room, but the fact that he knew how to use it. He had a way of lifting his head and pitching his voice up to the domed ceiling so that it carried his words to every part of the amphitheatre. He knew just how long to let each phrase fade to echoes before speaking the next.

'Like all the animals of the Forest, the fox lived without words,' Reynard said. 'He had no words and he needed none. He was there, and the Forest was there, and that was all he needed to know.

'But one day a new kind of life appeared in the Forest. This creature was different from any that had come before, because it had given itself a name.

'The new creature said: "I am a human being."'

'This interfering creature was not content with naming itself. It had to give names to everything it saw. It named every plant, every animal, every valley and hill. When it had finished naming, it began to make up stories. It looked at the fox, and it said: "The fox is cunning." It looked at the other animals of the Forest, and it said: "Wolves are savage. The cat is selfish. The mule is stubborn. The bear is strong."

'And the words of the human being had this curious power, that once they had been spoken they could not be undone. The fox found that he was cunning, just as the human said. He was no longer a creature without a name, free of meaning. Now the fox was a character in a story the human had made up.

'And so the fox realised he was a slave. There was no going back. He must live in the world of language that the human had invented and act out the stories that the human wanted to tell. From now on he would always be a creature of words.'

Reynard had been circling the arena as he told his story to the assembled foxes. Now he turned with a theatrical flourish to Silas, and let his voice resound across the Hall.

'You, Silas the human,' he said. 'When you had your little adventure with the wolves, did you think you were on the side of freedom? Did you believe you were helping brave survivors to escape from tyranny? No. You are the tyrant, human, and I am the slave. But I will win my freedom.

'You came here as our enemy, breaking the rules of hospitality that bind guest and host. But we welcome you, because this is a great day for all foxes. At last we can stand face to face with a human being and demand justice.'

He raised his voice, and the power that had been hidden in his words all along seemed only now to unfurl. Reynard's cry thundered as if the whole city of Earth were speaking.

'Justice for the wrongs you have done us!'

He turned from Silas and looked up at his audience. The foxes who packed the rows of seats from floor to ceiling were all in motion, as if the energy of Reynard's speech was vibrating through their bodies. They jostled in place, restless with doubt and excitement.

'I have brought this human before you, sisters and brothers, to show that his tyranny can be defeated. Humans are not our masters. We do not have to fear them. We do not have to be as they are.

'I declare that words no longer belong to humans. From this day forward, the words are ours. From now on, we foxes tell our own stories. Death to tyrants!'

Cheers rang out: the shrieks, barks and yelps of a great horde of creatures eager for action.

'Human child,' said Reynard. He was speaking more softly again, but his voice seemed to come from every part of the Hall. 'You are the enemy of the foxes and of all the animals of the Forest. For your crimes and the crimes of your species, you are condemned to death. Your sentence will be carried out at once, before the foxes of the city of Earth, who are gathered here to see justice done.'

The crowd yapped and barked, and Silas felt very exposed, standing alone on the bare sand.

'The fall of the tyrant means a new time of freedom and prosperity for foxes,' Reynard said. 'His punishment will fit his crimes. He helped our slaves in their rebellion, and so his death will show us their fresh obedience.'

Reynard lifted his paw to Isengrim and Hersent. They padded forward.

'Wolves,' Reynard said. 'You live to serve the foxes now, and your first task is to carry out the sentence I have passed. Tear the human to pieces.'

A murmur of excitement spread around the audience. This was a display they had not been expecting to see.

Silas wondered what was happening above the ground, in the human world, at his house. He tried to imagine Mum and Dad and Allie as they would be, right now: were they still crying and calling his name? Were they out searching for him? Had they got in trouble for losing him? Were they sure by now that he would never come home? He could not tell, could not begin to form a picture in his mind. None of it seemed real.

The wolves were real. They circled him. They were wild animals with heavy muscles and hard jaws made for tearing flesh and breaking bone. Silas turned back and forth, his feet scuffing the sand of the arena. There was nowhere for him to go.

It took him a minute to notice that the wolves were not coming any closer. After a while, their circling stopped. They stood with their ears flattened and their tails low. Silas did not know why they were delaying. He caught Isengrim's eyes, then Hersent's single eye, but he could not guess at the wolves' thoughts.

'How interesting!' Reynard said. 'Look closely, sisters and brothers, because here we see the simplicity of wolves. We see their need for the firm hand of a wiser species. Note how they hesitate to carry out the instruction I have given. They feel some loyalty to this human, and their poor wolfish brains are confused. They forget that the only purpose of a wolf is to obey the word of a fox without question or delay. In short, they need another lesson.'

Reynard signalled to his guards, who dragged the wolf pups into the arena. Two foxes held the pups by the scruffs of their necks, but the third fox shoved his pup to the ground, pinned her there and gripped her throat between his teeth. She was the smallest of the three pups, the one with fur paler than her sisters'.

'I will remind you one last time why you belong to the foxes,' Reynard said. 'My brother fox here only needs to squeeze a little tighter and it will be the end of this young wolf. Try to understand, because it's important: that is what will happen unless you carry out my order.'

Reynard strolled to the pup.

'I wonder if she realises?' he said, sniffing at her. 'Does she know her life depends on what her parents do now?'

It seemed to Silas that the wolves stood there for a long time, and that when they turned away from their pups and came towards him, they came slowly. But they were padding closer, and there was no doubt in their eyes about what was next.

Silas supposed his mind should be racing now: working faster than it had ever worked before, to come up with some plan, invent some way to escape. But he could not think. The wolves were coming. His mind was dry sand. All he knew was that the wolves had no choice, and neither did he.

He knelt down and closed his eyes. He was trembling. Curious ideas came and went. The further off things were, he thought, the bigger they looked. He felt that all the space in the world was held in this body, kneeling here with eyes closed. He felt that all the time in the world was in the few seconds that were left.

He waited for the wolves.

Then he opened his eyes.

'I know,' he said.

Wolf breath was hot on his face.

'I think ... I get it,' he said. 'Yes. I see the mistake Reynard's made.'

The scent of wolves filled his nostrils. Dry earth when rain falls.

'He says you have to choose between death and slavery for your children. He thinks your love for your pups makes you frightened, and that your fear gives him power over you.'

Silas was speaking slowly, finding out what he wanted to say even as the words came.

'But ... that's his mistake. He's thinking like a human being. He knows that if a human has to make that decision, they're trapped. They'll give up their freedom so they can live, or perhaps they'll choose to die instead, but either way they have no way out of the choice. That's how it is for humans. But he's forgotten wolves don't work that way.'

Silas kept expecting to stumble and fall silent, but with every word his voice was growing stronger and surer.

'Hersent, don't you remember what you said about hunting? When a wolf kills a deer, there isn't a winner or a loser, because those are human words and they mean nothing to the hunter or the prey. This is like that. It's the same.'

He paused, not hurrying, getting his thoughts clear. Isengrim and Hersent were not the only ones listening. Every one of the thousands of animals in the Hall was silent and attentive. Remembering how Reynard had pitched his voice into the roof, he tried doing the same, and his words resounded back to him, expanding to fill the space.

'Reynard taught you so many words that he got you to believe you were trapped by them,' he told the wolves. 'But the truth is that you can't make a wolf choose between slavery and freedom, or between life and death, because those are words, and words are human things, and they mean nothing to wolves.'

He paused and breathed deep, certain now that he could say what he wanted to say. He called to the furthest reaches of the Great Hall, and heard his voice ring out as clearly as Reynard's ever had.

'Wolves don't win or lose. They aren't masters or slaves. Wolves aren't right or wrong, they aren't good or bad, they aren't brave or frightened, they aren't strong or weak, they aren't free or captive. They're wolves. And words can't tell them what they mean.'

Isengrim and Hersent stood over him, still listening, although he had said everything he could think of. Then something in their eyes changed.

'We're wolves,' Isengrim said. 'We had forgotten.'

They fell back from Silas and circled towards Reynard.

'We're wolves,' said Hersent. 'And we will not do as you say.'

Reynard sighed.

'Oh, for goodness' sake,' he said. 'Really? Very well, then.'

He nodded to the guard holding down the smallest pup. The pale-furred wolf wriggled, mewling with fear, but she could not break free of the jaws at her throat.

'Kill it,' he said.

'Hurt that pup and you die,' Silas said, not missing a beat. His voice was steady. He knew what to say now. As he spoke, he got to his feet. 'You can kill her, but you won't live long enough to take another breath. This wolf will make sure of that.'

The fox hesitated. The pup's throat was between his teeth, but Hersent was ready to spring.

'That's a promise. Whatever else happens, the wolves promise that if you harm the pup, you die,' Silas said. 'Are you ready for that, brother fox? Is it worth your while?'

The fox's gaze shifted from Silas to Hersent to Reynard. With an apologetic twitch of his tail, he let go of the pup.

'How dare you!' Reynard said. 'I gave an order!'

The fox backed to the edge of the arena, as far from

the wolves as he could get, and glanced at the doorway the prisoners had come in by.

'This is insubordination,' Reynard said. His voice was calm. 'If you think you have more to fear from these wolves than you do from me, you're making a bad mistake.'

He pointed at the fox holding the second pup. Her angular eyes were wide with fright.

'You,' he said. 'Kill that whelp, if you know what's good for you.'

'He threatens,' Silas said. 'But the wolves make you a promise. Hurt the pup and you die.'

This fox did not hesitate as long as the other. He let go of the pup and backed away.

'Traitors!' snarled Reynard. 'Very well, then. You —'

But even as he spoke, the third guard was letting go of the pup and following his comrades. The three foxes eyed the doorway out of the arena. Then, all at once, they fled. Ripples of astonishment ran around the audience as the gathered foxes tried to make sense of what they had just seen.

Hersent bounded to her pups. They crowded between her legs and she stood over them four-square, defying all the foxes in the world to try and touch them again.

Silas was still standing in the arena, and the tiers of foxes still stared down, but they were no longer staring at him. They were watching Reynard, and they were watching Isengrim as he advanced on the fox.

Behind Reynard, the ranks of his guards shuffled their paws. He rounded on them.

'What are you waiting for?' he shouted. 'You should be ashamed to wear those collars!'

Isengrim was close, but Reynard barely seemed to notice.

'Let me be clear,' he said to the guards. 'These wolves are vermin. We've tried to improve them, but they can't be helped. So they are to be wiped out – right now. That's an order. Any fox of the guard who disobeys is going to wish his punishment was as easy as a traitor's death.'

Reynard ducked away as Isengrim's jaws clicked shut an inch from his nose. The fox's golden eyes were bright with rage.

'Do you hear me?' he said. 'GET HIM!'

The guards shook themselves. Silas moved closer to Hersent and the pups as the foxes surrounded Isengrim. They were much smaller, but there were dozens of them, snapping at the old wolf from every side. If they all attacked at once, Isengrim would surely be overwhelmed – but the foxes were hanging back. None of them wanted to be the first to come in range of Isengrim's jaws.

At last, one fox lunged. Isengrim caught him, shook him once and flung him over the heads of the others. The body thumped into the sand. Isengrim showed bloody teeth and snarled.

The foxes of the guard shrank from the dark, bristling form of the wolf. Then their line broke and they ran after their comrades. Within moments the last had vanished through the doorway. The only foxes left in the arena were Todd, astonished to find he was no longer a prisoner, and Reynard.

In the banks of seats, the foxes of the city were in uproar. Those close to the arena were scrambling to get away from the wolves. Those higher up were fighting towards the exits, but every aisle was blocked with panicking animals. The Great Hall rang with shouts and shrieks, building to such a confusion of echoes that by now the whole domed roof was roaring.

At the centre of the chaos, Isengrim stood over Reynard. The fox sat as neatly and calmly as he had sat on the cycle path the first time Silas had seen him.

'What are you waiting for?' he said to Isengrim. 'Do you expect me to say you've won, just because you've chased away those cowards? That wolves deserve their freedom after all? Do you want me to plead for mercy?'

Foxes do not smile, but Reynard grinned a hard grin.

'Sorry to disappoint.'

He went for Isengrim's throat. But before his jaws could find their target, the wolf's paw knocked him to the ground. The fox staggered to his feet, making an odd movement with his mouth. One of his canine teeth lay in the sand.

Reynard the fox took one unsteady step sideways. He licked at the broken place where his tooth had been. He narrowed his eyes at the wolf. Then he turned tail, ran for the door, and was gone.

15

WHILE THE foxes fought in the upper circles of the Hall, the survivors came together in the arena below: Silas, Todd, Hersent, Isengrim and the pups. The voices of the frightened animals seemed to swirl around the bowl-shaped room, turning it into a whirlpool of noise. Then Silas heard a new sound through the din.

'*Kraa*! *Kraa*!'

Corax the raven was flapping through the upper air of the Hall. She had flown in by an entrance at the top. Now she swooped down to the arena and landed in a flurry of black wings.

'I was wrong,' she said. 'Shouldn't have done it. So I went to find him, and I told him what happened.'

New screams came from the foxes who had not yet escaped the Hall. Another animal was coming through that upper entrance. The frame of the door cracked. It was as if a huge brown boulder had come to life and was forcing its way in. He looked larger and more powerful than ever. Bruno the bear.

Foxes bit and clawed one another to get away from him, but he ignored them. He lumbered down the rows of seats as if he were alone in the room.

'Bruno!' Isengrim called, but the bear did not seem to hear. He was heading for one of the four stone pillars that held up the ceiling. When he reached the pillar, he reared up on his hind legs and threw his front paws around it. He roared, and was answered by a grinding noise from above. Dust began to pour from the ceiling.

'Oh,' said Hersent.

'Ah,' said Isengrim.

'What?' said Todd. His mouth hung open.

The bear roared and strained. It seemed impossible that the pillar could fall: it was built of stone blocks joined with mortar, and it was broader across than Bruno himself. But the bear braced against the seats and drove his body into the stone, bellowing with effort, until, slowly, it shifted. The fall of dust grew faster and the pillar made a mighty cracking noise. Then it toppled, crashing across the seats and turning a quarter of the Hall to wreckage. Rubble cascaded down. The screams of foxes were lost in the noise of tortured stone.

Corax flapped frantically.

'Where's Tybalt?'

Knocking aside chunks of masonry, the bear began to wade through the debris towards the second pillar.

'Where's the cat?'

'He didn't make it,' Hersent said. 'He fought the foxes, but there were too many.'

Corax's cry was a shriek of pain.

'Where is he?'

'The Keep,' Hersent said. 'You can't do anything, Corax. He's gone.'

The raven flew to the door at the edge of the arena.

'Need to see.'

Bruno reached the second pillar. He embraced the stone and leaned into it with all his weight. Another sluice of dust poured down.

'Those pillars don't just hold up this ceiling,' Isengrim said. 'They hold up the entire city.'

'We have to leave,' Hersent said.

The raven's head flicked back and forth. She looked at the door at the top of the aisle, leading to the Upper City and the surface. She looked at the door beside her, which led down to the Keep. Last of all, she looked at the wolves and at Silas, with an eye like a shiny black bead.

She flew through the door leading downwards.

Isengrim, Hersent and the wolf pups raced up the aisle, up the slope of the bowl-shaped room. Silas and Todd followed. Most of the foxes had gone, and those that were left shrank in terror from the wolves.

'No hiding now,' Isengrim said. 'We run for the surface.'

They looked down into the ruin of the Great Hall.

Isengrim called Bruno's name again, and the bear blinked up at them. He gave a nod and lifted his paw. He turned back to the pillar. He seemed to rest for a moment, gathering his strength; then he wrapped his forelegs around the stone and pushed. An enormous, jagged crack appeared in the ceiling.

Amid spurts of dust and the crackle of stone, Silas and his companions ran along streets and up spiral stairwells that shook as if they might buckle and fold. Tremors came from below. As he ran, Silas expected the buried city to collapse into a throat of sand and clay that would swallow them to the depths. They ran across rippling cobblestones and up tunnels whose inclines grew steeper as they went, through skewing arches, under fallen beams, and finally towards a point of light that first receded ahead but then came closer and spread and became a gateway filled with a pale glow that opened up around them so suddenly that it took Silas a few moments to understand that they had burst out to the fresh air.

He gasped and tasted the breath of a million trees.

In the clearing the wolf pups danced around their mother and father. Night had fallen in the Forest, and the treetops were dark against the sky. The stars were out. The moon was full.

As the last foxes scampered into the woods, a long, deep groan came from beneath the ground: a groan not from the throat of any animal, but from the throat of the earth. The hillside sagged, a cloud of pale dust rose and the gate to the city fell in on itself. Silas and his companions watched a while longer, but no one else came out. They had not seen Corax the raven or Bruno the bear.

Todd stood watching longest of all. At last he turned his back on the ruined city.

'Where will you go, fox?' Isengrim said.

The little fox was scruffier than ever, and one of his ears was bloody and torn, but he held his head high as he faced the wolf.

'I'm going after the other foxes,' he said. 'There were others who felt the same as me. Now we need to work together. I'll bet Reynard made it out of the Earth, and he'll soon be making new plans. So the rest of us need plans of our own. The city's gone, our old life is over, and it's up to us to decide what the foxes do next.'

He trotted across the clearing. Just before he reached the trees, he looked back at Silas and the wolves.

'Because what we were isn't what we're going to be.'

He disappeared among the shadows.

Silas and the wolves walked in woods made strange by moonlight. The trees were a tangle of silver and shadow. He felt as if he were walking through an endless room filled with old mirrors and shadowy doorways.

The pups played as they went, racing ahead, hiding and pouncing. When Silas had unfastened the leather collars from their necks they had whined with relief.

Isengrim and Hersent walked at a steady, untiring pace, one on each side of Silas.

'Is that the end?' he asked. 'Will the foxes leave you alone?'

'There's nothing they can do to us,' Isengrim said. 'It doesn't matter whether Reynard escaped or not. He

tricked us into the world of words once, but he can't do it again. Not now that we remember what it is to be a wolf.'

Ahead, the pup with dark-tipped ears ambushed her sisters and chased them around a tree until all three fell in a heap.

'We can't lose our names. We'll always be Isengrim and Hersent, just as you'll always be who your name says you are. But these pups have no names, and they never will. We'll make sure they live nameless, as wolves ought to live.'

'Are you really the last wolves in the Forest?' Silas said. 'The last there'll ever be?'

'Perhaps. Perhaps when our lives and the lives of our daughters are finished, that will be the end of our kind. But the truth is we don't know, because the Forest goes far and deep and no one knows all its secrets. Perhaps there are other wolves.'

'Will you look for them?'

'First the pups have to grow. But once they're grown, we'll travel. We'll go far and deep into the Forest, and perhaps we'll find others. Perhaps the wolves will carry on.'

They stopped walking. Silas looked around, startled. Somehow the mirrors and doors of the moonlight had shifted, and he was no longer surrounded by trees. He and the wolves stood between a steel fence, a hedge and a gate leading to a footpath. A street lamp shed its light on a wheelie bin.

'You can find your way home from here,' Isengrim said.

'Yes,' said Silas. 'I know where I am.'

It occurred to him that he had been speaking freely for the whole night walk through the Forest. But he did not give this much thought, because there seemed nothing remarkable about it. The pups crowded around him, wagging their tails.

'Thank you, Silas,' Hersent said. 'You spoke for the wolves when we needed it most. You spoke and made us free of the words. You were the Wolfstongue.'

She moved closer.

'I'm glad you were there.'

Silas did not know what to say, so he knelt and hugged Hersent, then Isengrim, throwing his arms around their necks and burying his hands in the dense fur of their manes. No less than on the day when he had first met the wolves, it was remarkable to be here with these living creatures, in the warmth of their bodies and their scent of woodland, earth and rain. The pups licked his face, prodding him with cold noses.

Silas stood up. Lights sheared across the street, dazzling him, as a car passed the end of the road.

'Maybe I'll see you again,' he said.

But the shadowy forms in front of him were no longer animals. They were only shadows that had fallen across the hedge and the fence in a way that suggested the shapes of wolves, if you looked at it that way. But now that he looked again, he could not see them, or even remember what he thought he had seen.

He was alone.

16

CHILDREN WALKED through the school gates in pairs and groups, chattering, arguing, gossiping, joking and laughing. As usual, Silas was hanging back until the crowd had thinned out and he could set off for home without anyone noticing him. He stood by the porch at the front of the school building, where he could watch and wait and keep out of the way.

Raised voices echoed across the yard. Three girls from the year above passed in front of Silas, deep in discussion.

A heavy hand fell on his shoulder.

'Silence,' said Richie Long. 'There you are.'

Silas moved to walk away, but Richie Long tightened his grip.

'Where are you going? I'm talking to you.'

Silas shook off the hand and started across the yard, but Richie Long's friends blocked his way. Heads turned. Even the girls from the year above looked up from their conversation.

'Come on, Silence. Let's give it one more try,' Richie Long said.

Silas gave up trying to escape and looked across the yard at the trees beyond the fence.

'Repeat after me,' said Richie Long. He grinned. 'My ... Name ... Is ... Suh-suh-suh-suh-suh-suh-SILENCE!'

Someone chuckled. Then someone else. A ripple of laughter passed around the yard. Silas said nothing.

'Oh, well,' Richie Long said. 'Never mind. We'll keep working on it tomorrow, mate.'

He gave Silas what might have looked like a friendly punch in the arm. Silas stumbled from the blow, pushed past Richie Long's friends and hurried blindly through the school gates.

He did not slow down until he was on the cycle path, but as he came to the wire fence he found he was too tired to keep going. His stomach ached and he could feel a bruise coming up on his arm, among the older bruises. Richie Long and his friends were making fun of him every single break time, and he could not do anything about it. A few times he had tried to talk back, to stand up for himself, but his voice had seized up and no words had come. By now he had given up trying.

What was the point? That night, two whole months ago now, as he had walked back to his house after saying goodbye to the wolves, he had believed that something had changed inside himself. That his adventure in the city of the foxes must have made him into a new person, one who would now always be able to find the right words when he needed them. But it was not so. It was as if the time with the wolves had made no difference to who he was in his life.

When he had got home that night it had been long past midnight, but all the lights had been on in the house. He had found his parents and his sister in the living room. Among the broken furniture and the stains and scars left by the foxes, his family was sitting on the floor in a nest of cushions and blankets, Allie curled up, Mum and Dad holding on to one another, barely awake. When Silas walked in, they spent a long time staring at him, as if they had forgotten how to tell what was real and what was not. Then they had leaped at him with cries so loud and strange that he was frightened. Allie woke up and joined Mum and Dad squeezing him so hard that he could not even struggle. He could not tell if it was the worst thing that had ever happened or the best. It felt like both. Mum and Dad kept asking questions that he could not take in, let alone answer. Eventually they grew a little calmer and told one another to give him time and let him rest. Later he was aware of them talking on the phone and arguing with someone who came to the door, but by then he was curled in the warm nest on the floor with Allie's arm across him, and he was asleep.

In the days that followed, Mum and Dad would not take their eyes off him. He did not know whether they were angry or anxious, happy or sad, but he could tell they badly wanted him to say what had happened, why he had vanished and where he had been. He told them that all the damage to the house had been his doing, and that he had gone away of his own accord, that no-one else was to blame. But that was all he could manage. He could not explain where he had gone or what the reasons were. He could not begin to tell them about the wolves.

For several weeks Dad insisted on walking Silas to school every day and meeting him at the gate at home time. One afternoon, on the cycle path, Dad did a lot of throat-clearing and mumbling, and then told Silas that he and Mum were very sorry. They were sorry they hadn't known he was having a hard time and that they had not given him the help he needed. More than anything, they wanted to help. They just needed to know what was going on with him. But they knew it was difficult for him to talk, and they were not going to hurry him. They would give him time.

Silas was glad of this, but it was tiring to have Dad beside him, pained and patient, waiting for him to get around to explaining what was wrong. Eventually it got so tiring that Silas asked if he could go back to walking to and from school by himself, and his parents uneasily agreed.

And that was it. He could not see how anything was going to be different from now on. Mum and Dad were waiting for him to speak, but he would never be able to tell them what they wanted to know. He could not begin to explain about the wolves and the foxes and the Forest, any more than he could tell them about the way things were at school or about Richie Long and the others or the way that the words would not come when he needed them. Nothing had changed. What was the point?

His eyes prickled. He walked along the cycle path, squeezing his hand into a fist in the pocket of his jacket. Then he tore the fist out of the pocket and punched the wall. He yelped at the pain and stopped walking to examine the blood oozing from his knuckles.

He touched the wall, feeling the bite of the brick. He had never looked closely at this wall before, but now, with his knuckles stinging, he looked. He saw that each brick was a tiny landscape of ridges, peaks, rifts, pits and plains. No two were alike. The bricks and the gaps between them were home to many different kinds of life: clumps of moss, streaks of algae and blotches of lichen, and grass, nettles and small wildflowers growing in the cracks. Silas saw a caterpillar there too, and an ant; a whole column of ants climbing.

The wall was not just a wall, he realised. It was a tiny world in itself, and the closer you looked at it, the more you discovered. It was like looking into the night sky and finding stars in the darkness. Perhaps everything was like that, he thought. You will never reach the end, because the more you look, the more you find, on and on, for ever.

The Forest is everywhere, Isengrim had told him. You can find routes into it wherever you choose to look for them. And now that he looked, he saw it. Right beside him, a passage with walls of mossy brick.

He did not have to go down there, he told himself. He could carry on walking home. Perhaps that would be best, because of course things were not really so bad. At least they were not as bad as they could be. Perhaps it had just been wrong of him to expect anything ever to change.

He stood on the path for a minute, trying to make up his mind.

His feet stirred dead leaves. He clambered over big dry branches that blocked the passageway. He kept walking as the walls drew closer together and the moss thickened so that no more bricks could be seen. And then he was out of the passage, and into somewhere else.

He walked among big trees. He pushed under curtains of fern and made footprints in waterlogged moss. He did not know how long or how far he walked. Human troubles seemed less important with every step he took into the enormous silence of the Forest.

At last he saw shapes moving among the trees. Five grey shapes that loped silently towards him.

'Hello, Silas,' said Hersent. 'We thought you might come.'

———◆———

He walked with the wolves. They walked in green twilight, among twisted trunks, under tangled branches. Bracken brushed their legs. He put out a hand and touched the mane of the young wolf whose fur was paler than her sisters'. Her shoulder was as high as his waist: in the months since he had seen them, the young wolves had grown to twice the size they had been. They were not much smaller than their parents, though they still moved with puppyish lightness.

'You know your way through the Forest now,' Isengrim said.

'Sort of. I think I know how to get here.'

Silas frowned.

'No, that's not right. Getting here isn't the point. What I mean is, I used to think it must be about finding the way between one world and another. But that was wrong, because there's only one world.'

'Is that so?' said Isengrim, sounding amused.

'I thought you had to work out how to get to the Forest, but actually there's nothing to work out. You just look closely, and you see.'

'So you'll come and go as you please,' Isengrim said. 'But why have you come to us today?'

Silas pushed his hands into his pockets.

'Nothing's changed,' he said. 'When I was with you, I thought I could speak. I thought I'd learned. Listen to me: I'm doing it now. I can speak, but only when I'm here. At home it's still as hard as ever.'

The three young wolves ran into the trees ahead. Low sunlight had opened a shaft through the foliage. Dust and seeds swirled in the light. Leaves glowed.

The young wolves chased one another to a place where an angle of stone stuck up from the forest floor. It was a piece of ruin, swamped in sunlight and buried in ivy.

'Look,' Silas said, as they caught up with the pups. 'I know this place.'

He lifted a mat of ivy, revealing a mischievous stone face with carved leaves sprouting from its cheeks, chin and eyebrows. The face grinned up at Silas as if it had known everything that would happen, all along.

'I remember him,' Silas said.

He touched the stone face, thinking of a time when he had raced through the woodland, soaked in mud and frozen by rain, with wolves beside him and foxes behind.

'Silas,' said Hersent. 'You've heard the story of the Wolfstongue. But you haven't heard all of it. There's another part to the legend.'

She nudged Isengrim.

'You can tell it.'

'All right, then,' Isengrim said. 'Here's the story.

'Once, when the Forest was young, there lived a child. This child was not like other human children, because he could not speak for himself as they did. Words to him were pain and trouble. They did not come easily, and often he wept in his heart because he could not say what he needed to say.

'But pain and trouble bring understanding, which ease does not. By struggling so long and so hard with the words, the child came to know the power that was in them, and the danger. He knew the hurt that words could do to those who must live in silence.

'The wolves lived in silence, and when they saw the child, they knew him. He was a Wolfstongue child. He knew what it was to live in silence, and this meant he could speak for the wolves. Words had hurt the wolves, trapped them in prison and put them to death, and so they asked the child for his help. They asked him to speak his words for them. And the child gave the wolves the help they needed. He spoke for them so that they could live free in their silence.

'Once the wolves were free, the Wolfstongue child went back to the humans, but his pain and trouble were not over. Human words hurt him, because they spoke in cruelties and lies, and he wept in his heart. He saw that humans could never be free from the prisons they built with their words.

'And so, just as he had given the wolves the gift of his language, the wolves offered him the gift of their silence. They told the child that if he chose, he could leave the world of words, where the humans live, and go to live where there are no words and none are needed.

'He would become a wolf.'

Hersent pushed her head into the palm of Silas's hand. He looked down at the long white scar.

'If you want to, you can join us,' she said.

Silas let the ivy fall over the stone face. *Join us.* He wondered what it would mean. He squatted and looked at the ground between his feet. He parted the ivy and found the earth. He dug his fingers into the soil and lifted a handful towards his face.

This was not magic clay from the heart of the earth, the dark stuff from which life is moulded. This was just a handful of ordinary soil. But it was cold and heavy in his hand, and as he looked into it he began to see twinkling specks, like stars that only looked small because they were so impossibly far away. He breathed the cold smell of the earth, and he felt the earth's dreams in his hand. He felt what it would be like to change his shape and become a wolf.

The late afternoon light burned in the branches.

'I can't,' he said. 'I'd miss my family, and they'd be sad without me. And I have to sort stuff out at school too.'

As he said this, it did not seem too much to cope with.

They walked on.

The sun dipped and the woods filled with shadow. In the distance a bell had started clanging. A slow, steady beat of iron on iron, sounding small and lonely through the trees.

They drew closer to the sounding of the bell and came to a place where the big trees ended in a stretch of grass edged with flowerbeds. Silas saw paved paths, iron railings and the glass dome of a tropical plant house. They were in the park in the middle of town. The keeper was ringing the bell to let people know that soon the park would be closing for the night.

'It would be good to be a wolf,' Silas said. 'But I'm a human, and I need to speak to other humans. I have things to tell them.'

The wolves stood under the trees as Silas started across the grass. He looked back and raised his hand. Already

they were grey shadows, and their eyes were green points of light.

The bell clanged. The wolves watched from the trees as the child walked away, heading out of the park, going deeper into the world.

We hope you have enjoyed reading *Wolfstongue*. On the following pages you will find an interview with the author, Sam Thompson, as well as some information about other Little Island titles you might like to read.

Little Island Books

www.littleisland.ie

AN INTERVIEW WITH AUTHOR SAM THOMPSON

SIOBHÁN PARKINSON is the author of more than thirty books for children, teens and adults, in Irish and English, and she has translated a number of books from German. She was Ireland's first ever Laureate na nÓg (children's laureate). In 2010 she founded Little Island Books. Here she talks to SAM THOMPSON about *Wolfstongue* and what he is writing next.

Sam, tell us a little bit about your life. When and where do you do your writing, and do you find inspiration in the world around you?

I'm from England but I live in Belfast with my wife Caoileann, our children Oisín, Odhrán and Sadhbh, and a very un-wolf-like cockapoo called Suky. My perfect writing scenario is that I get to go into my little study and write for a couple of hours every day. I find lots of inspiration in knowing that the busy life of our household is going on just outside the door.

Did you always want to be a writer, even as a child? What kinds of books did you like to read when you were young?

When I was small the idea of 'being a writer' never exactly occurred to me, but I was always serious about reading. So many books made a permanent impression, from Jan Pienkowski's *Haunted House* and Maurice Sendak's *Where The Wild Things Are* to Terry Jones's *Erik The Viking* and Tony Robinson's retelling of the story of Odysseus; then *Treasure Island*, Rosemary Sutcliffe's *The Eagle of the Ninth*, Joan Aiken's *The Wolves of Willoughby Chase*, Ursula Le Guin's Earthsea books, John Christopher's Tripods trilogy, Calvin and Hobbes, the Molesworth series by Geoffrey Willans and Ronald Searle. If you asked me tomorrow I'd give you a whole different list. All the books you read come together in the imaginary library in your head, and no one else's library is quite the same as yours.

Wolfstongue **is your first children's book, but you've written a couple of books for adults too. Do you find writing for children very different from writing for adults?**

It doesn't really feel different, because whatever I'm writing, I'm trying to tell the story in the simplest and truest way I can. To begin with I'm just writing for myself, hoping that if I can make the story ring true for me then the same will happen for others when they read it. The only difference with *Wolfstongue* was that I often felt I was writing not for my grown-up self, but for myself as a child – and somehow this made it seem extra-important to tell the story right.

This story is not set in any particular place – it could be anywhere. In your head, what kind of place does Silas live in?

I started writing *Wolfstongue* when I was living in Oxford and finished it after moving to Belfast, and the town where Silas lives is a mixture of the two. I've explored both cities with my children, and doing so has helped me understand that cities don't belong only to human beings. Humans build cities for themselves, but once a city is built it becomes just another part of the natural world – an environment we share with other forms of life which flourish in the gaps we leave. That's the kind of place where Silas lives.

This is a story about humans and animals, but it's also about being a boy in the modern world, at school, part of a family, struggling with various things. What made you want to write about those ideas?

Stories often come into existence when two separate ideas bump into one another. With *Wolfstongue* it was my son Odhrán who gave me the connection. He was about five years old, and he was having some trouble with his speech. He liked to draw wolves and make up stories about them, and he used to march about shouting 'I AM A GOOD WOLF!' So I was thinking a lot about being a boy in the modern world, and about speech and words and the ways they can be difficult – but at the same time I was thinking about wolves, and I began to feel that all these things were linked. I had an instinct that I could make some sense of them all by putting them in a story together.

Were you influenced by old stories about foxes and wolves in writing this book?

Yes! Humans have always used animals to tell stories about ourselves. The stories that mainly influenced this book are a set of fables from medieval Europe about Reynard the Fox, a trickster who always gets the better of the other animals, especially Isengrim the Wolf. Isengrim has such a hard time in those stories that I wanted to see if I could give him a better ending!

Wolves are usually the baddies in folk tales and children's stories, but in this book, they are definitely the animals the reader likes. What made you want to make wolves the 'goodies'?

Sometimes new stories come from the urge to flip old ones upside-down.

In the medieval tales of Reynard the Fox it's not that Reynard is good and Isengrim is bad, but that Reynard is clever while Isengrim is stupid. Tricksters are usually the heroes of their tales, because we love to hear about wily fellows who can break the rules and always come out on top. But I wanted to write a story about the ones who get tricked by the trickster – because that's most of us, at least some of the time.

In this book, using his own voice is problematic for Silas; for the foxes, using language has made them more like humans; and for the wolves, language is something they want to distance themselves from. These are difficult

ideas but they work very well in the story. How did you manage that?

We are all shaped by the language we use and the language others use about us. Silas, the foxes and the wolves all have their own struggle with language, so those ideas about words naturally came out of telling what happens with these characters.

The stories we tell can grow so powerful that they transform reality. For example, the idea that wolves are monsters that we should hate and fear. It's true that wolves can be dangerous to humans, but humans are even more dangerous to wolves. We are the only creatures who can tell stories about how wolves are the enemy and then work together to destroy them, as happened in Ireland, where the last wolf was killed around 250 years ago.

Who would you say is the real hero of this story? Is it Silas or Isengrim?

It depends what you mean by 'hero'. Silas is the one we follow through the story, the human traveller who goes into the world of the animals. That makes him a hero, but part of his adventure is discovering that it's not all about him. The wolves are the heroes of their own story. Each of us is the hero of our own tale, and everyone around us is a hero to themselves. Even Reynard is the hero of his own story.

By the end of the book, Silas has learnt a lot, but he hasn't solved all his problems, and neither have the wolves solved theirs. I think there is going to be a sequel. Can you give us just a tiny hint about how the second story will develop?

Yes. After finishing this book, I found I still had questions. What is the magic clay and what else can it do? Where will the wolves go as they travel deeper into the Forest, and will Silas see them again? And what other plans does Reynard have up his sleeve? He's not the sort of fox to give up easily: he may have lost his underground city, but he has something much bigger planned next ...

Thank you, Sam!

Coming in 2022 from Little Island

THE FOX'S TOWER

by SAM THOMPSON
Illustrated by ANNA TROMOP

THE SEQUEL TO *Wolfstongue*

Thirty years have passed since Silas first entered the Forest and helped his wolf friends in their struggle with the foxes. Silas is grown now but his daughter, Willow, will be the next child to enter the hidden world of the Forest: the next Wolfstongue.

Publishing in 2022
ISBN: 978-1-912417-92-6

THE WORDSMITH
by PATRICIA FORDE

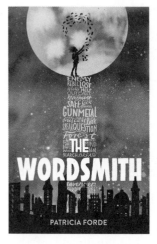

Letta loves her job as the Wordsmith's apprentice, giving out words to people who need them. It doesn't strike her as odd that the people of Ark are only allowed to use a few hundred words, and words like 'love', 'hope' and 'freedom' are banned.

When her master disappears, Letta starts to understand that all is not well – John Noa, the ruler of Ark, is out to destroy language altogether. Letta has to find a way to stop him silencing what is left of the human race.

But she's only a young girl, and he's the leader of the known world ...

'The fantasy book of the year.' – Eoin Colfer

'A novel that truly stands apart for its originality and relevance ... a book about words, about language, about their power to civilise – and, in the wrong hands, to abuse and dehumanise.' – *The Irish Times*

**WINNER OF A WHITE RAVEN AWARD
FROM THE INTERNATIONAL YOUTH LIBRARY**

MOTHER TONGUE
by PATRICIA FORDE

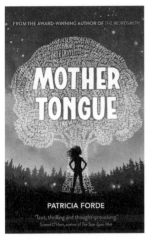

The sequel to
The Wordsmith

After Global Warming came The Melting. Then came Ark. Letta is the wordsmith, tasked with keeping words alive. Out in the woods, she and the rebels secretly teach children language, music and art.

Now there are rumours that babies are going missing. When Letta makes a horrifying discovery, she has to find a way to save the children of Ark – even if it is at the cost of her own life.

'Subtle, humane and inspiring. An amazing book.' – Anne Booth, author of *Across the Divide*

'Totally enthralling ... a world where the horror of climate change has been realised but despite the despair, the hope of humanity lives on.' – *The Book Activist*

GOLD
by GERALDINE MILLS

Esper and Starn live in a grim world that has been almost laid waste by massive volcanic explosions. Very little grows in Orchard, which used to be a fruit-growing area, but with the death of insects and birds, pollination of the fruit trees is a precarious undertaking.

When the boys discover an intriguing old manuscript in a locked room in their apartment, which tells of gold on one of the forbidden islands the people can see from the coastline, they determine to go on gold-hunt.

'The twins' quick-paced, action-packed journey will sweep readers right along with them.' – *Kirkus Reviews*, starred review

MY SECRET DRAGON
by DEBBIE THOMAS

Aidan Mooney has the mother of all problems. His mum is part-dragon.

He's spent his whole life struggling to keep her hidden from the world. But now, with the help of his super-smart new friend Charlotte, Aidan discovers a much darker secret hiding in the woods ...

Loneliness, isolation, anxiety and being different are explored in this tender and heartwarming tale.

'A smashing romp. The writing is excellent.'
– Celine Kiernan, author of *Begone the Raggedy Witches*

'Unforgettable characters and page-turning action.'
– ER Murray, author of the Book of Learning trilogy

ACKNOWLEDGEMENTS

All my love and thanks to Caoileann, always, all over again. James, Andrew, Jane, Alec and Carey, Dan and Jenny: thank you for your love and support and for being this book's loyal pack. Thank you, Mima and Windsor, Toby and Pippa, Lily, Holly, Jim and Bernie.

For friendship, advice, guidance, encouragement and opportunity, thank you: Michelle Ryan, Ronan Crowley, Amanda Piesse, Deborah Friedell, Bryan Radley, Darran McCann, Caspar Henderson, Myra Zepf, Emma Quigley, Kelly McCaughrain, Mark Richards, Chris Priest, Nina Allan, Damian Smyth.

Thanks to Eleanor Birne and all at PEW Literary. Thanks to Siobhán Parkinson, Matthew Parkinson-Bennett, Elizabeth Goldrick, Aurélie Connan and all at Little Island. Thanks to Anna Tromop for her wonderful illustrations.

Sadhbh, Odhrán, Oisín: thank you for everything. This story is yours.

ABOUT LITTLE ISLAND BOOKS

Little Island publishes good books for young minds, from toddlers to teens. Based in Dublin, Ireland, Little Island specialises in Irish writers and also publishes some works in translation. It is Ireland's only English-language publisher that specialises in books for young readers, and receives funding from the Arts Council of Ireland.

www.littleisland.ie

RECENT AWARDS FOR LITTLE ISLAND BOOKS

Savage Her Reply by Deirdre Sullivan
WINNER: YA Book of the Year, An Post Irish Book Awards 2020

The Deepest Breath by Meg Grehan
WINNER: Judges' Special Prize, KPMG Children's Books Ireland Awards 2020
SHORTLISTED: Waterstones Children's Book Prize 2020

Mucking About by John Chambers
Selected for the IBBY Honours List 2020

123 Ireland! by Aoife Dooley
WINNER: Children's Book of the Year (Junior), An Post Irish Book Awards 2019

Bank by Emma Quigley
WINNER: The Literacy Association of Ireland Children's Book Award 2019

Dangerous Games by James Butler
WINNER: The Great Reads Award 2019

Dr Hibernica Finch's Compelling Compendium of Irish Animals by Aga Grandowicz and Rob Maguire
WINNER: Honour Award for Illustration, Children's Books Ireland Awards 2019

Little Island Books